The Saundersfoot Suicides

Andrew Peters

Cover art by the wonderful Joe Lumley
joe-lumley@live.co.uk

Talk to me

andynpeters@yahoo.com

DISCLAIMER

This book has been compiled from interview tapes with ex-Chief Superintendent Williams, and has not been edited in any way.

No checking for accuracy has been possible, since it appears that Mr Williams has changed all names, places, dates and events to suit himself.

It is entirely possible that he invented the whole story.

Spaz

There can't be many nastier words in any language. Go on, say it. Not just quietly, nice and loud, as if you were hurling it at someone you despised. Go on. Give it plenty of effort.

First of all you'll need to hiss the 'S' enough to make it sound menacing, then give full value to the 'P'. It's a plosive, so make it bloody well explode. You'll need your mouth wide open for the 'A', of course, and narrow your eyes a little, see if you can make the veins on your neck stand out some. Then finally pull back the corners of your mouth and stick your teeth together for the 'Z'. Apparently that's a fricative, so you can keep making that rubbing, hissing noise for a bit.

A horrible word. Even if you didn't speak a word of English, you'd know it was abuse. It could never be confused with some word meaning 'beautiful' or 'flower' or 'love'.

It sounds vile and it is vile.

And that's before you even get to the meaning.

You've probably seen them, if you ever go to the beach in summer they're usually taken there for an outing. You can see them in the little buses with 'Spastics Society' painted on the side. Most people look away when their keepers help them out. Poor sods can hardly walk, some of them with their arms flailing about, others mooing like demented cows. I'm told it depends which part of their brain is damaged. Maybe at birth, maybe before birth, I'm no doctor. Poor sods.

And that's what they used to call me.

A spastic.

The Spaz.

It's a funny thing about school, it's pretty much the last time in your life that you'll find yourself judged by what you CAN'T do rather than by what you can. Makes no difference how good you are at English, French and Latin...what your report will always pick up on is the weaknesses. 'He needs to work harder at his Maths if he is to improve his overall level'. You can win the school music prize, but the headmaster will still be keen to point out to your parents your lack of progress in bloody history. As if anyone needs to see Artur Rubenstein's bloody science marks.

But of all the things that you'd better not stink at, for Christ's sake don't be bad at games. Really. If you're having trouble with almost any other subject, the teachers will help you. They'll come over to your desk and explain Pythagoras's theorem just one more time, point out those verb mistakes or even show you what Shakespeare really meant.

PE and games? Forget it.

They'll give up on you on Day One, when it

becomes obvious that your stomach is hanging over your gym shorts, you can't climb a rope or do a cartwheel to save your life and you can't catch a rugby ball without your glasses, especially when the big tough kids are charging down at you.

"Passmore, pay attention"

"Passmore, what's the matter with you?"

"Passmore, can't you do the simplest thing?"

Well no, Passmore couldn't. Passmore was a poor little short-sighted fat bugger, easy to pick on. Passmore was twelve years old, beginning to develop spots and really not growing as big as the other boys, many of whom needed a shave. Passmore liked English and Latin and generally showed up as late as possible for games in the hope that neither side would want him. Passmore desperately wanted to be good at games, but couldn't manage it.

That was me, Passmore. Quentin Stanley Passmore. Yeah, I might just as well have had a target tattooed on my forehead. Quentin, for Christ's sake. Then S Passmore. Just shoot me now. Of course, If I'd been large and sporty, I'd have got away with it and made it fashionable, but a little fat specky sod? I think not.

Well, maybe it was nobody's fault. The Quentin came from my father who was blown to bits over Hamburg before I was even born. Stanley was my grandfather, who I also never knew. Passmore was the family name, which mother didn't see fit to change, even after she remarried.

Not that I had anything against the new husband, as stepfathers go he went pretty well I suppose. Certainly no mistreatment and provided for us well, though mother always held her end up professionally. Just that I wasn't his, I was something he had to put up with if he wanted my mother. Plenty of money then, but bugger all understanding from either of them of what I was going through.

Of course, that might have been because I never told either of them about it. Well, you didn't. It would have been sneaking, wouldn't it? And there was nothing worse than sneaking, was there? Not even making some poor bugger wish he was dead every day for six years. So I kept my trap shut.

"How were things at school today, Quentin?"

"Oh fine, mum."

And that was as far as it went. No call for them to worry, since my report always made happy reading. Except for sport and PE of course.

"Passmore needs to put in more effort, he is lazy and lacks co-ordination. Needs to lose weight."

No, Spaz Passmore really wasn't up to the physical stuff, and there was bugger all he could do about it. So he tried plan B. He became the funny man.

It wasn't all that hard, because Passmore was a damned sight more intelligent than most of the bastards. He could watch the TV and remember jokes, he used to buy joke books, and he was much faster and wittier than the rest of them. So he kept them amused, and kept himself out of trouble most of the time. He was clever enough never to come top of the form and attract attention. About third would usually be good enough to satisfy the parents and not upset the tough boys.

But still there'd be the big lads at games time.

"Oi...Spaz...over 'ere...on me 'ead," as I desperately chased a ball towards the touchline.

"Spaz, tackle 'im," as some six foot thug charged down at me.

And then the inevitable "Awwwwwww...Spaz."

The teachers really were no help at all. They couldn't actually call me 'Spaz' but it came bloody close. "Rubbishsss Passmore" "Don't miss the tacklesss Passmore". It's like the old saying goes, 'Those who can, do. Those who can't, teach. Those who can't teach, teach sports'.

There were games I could actually play, if they could have given a shit.

Cricket.

Well, I couldn't bat and I was too fat and uncoordinated to field, but I was a shit-hot spin bowler. Not that anyone ever noticed. In my fifth year I showed up for every cricket practice for three months, and only got a game on the day that everyone else was doing Science resits. Milford Grammar School were 180-1 when they tossed me the ball as a joke. Twenty minutes later they were all out for 228 and I'd taken 7-22. Made bugger-all difference, we still lost by 110 runs and I was last out.

"Awwwww....Spaz!" As if you'd expect the number eleven batsman to score a century

It wasn't a bad school. I learned a lot, but the traditional ideas buggered me up. It was bad enough for the first five years, but once we got to the sixth form things got much worse.

That's when the girls came in.

It was a popular thing in those days, once a school reached the sixth form stage in came the girls.

Did me no good at all. Everyone else was six foot tall and shaving, there was the Spaz, still wearing his puppy fat and swotting up his Latin. Girls of sixteen and a little fat sod? It was never going to happen. So much blonde hair and breasts and I was still reading Batman comics. They weren't usually unkind to me, just treated me as a puppy. A rather amusing funny puppy. The sixth form men didn't see me as a threat. Of course not. I was just The Spaz.

I stuck it out through the lower sixth form. I was a

year younger than most of them, since the sportsboys had taken an extra year to do their O levels. But I was still a kid in a class full of adults. Until I reached the June of the lower sixth.

I'd been careless, got carried away with enjoying the work and actually won the form prize. As a matter of fact it didn't seem to be a big thing for anybody. Never even told my parents. It got me carried away for almost a week until they started selling tickets for the school dance. Meant to be for the sixth form, but the big guys from the fifth and the important people from the upper sixth were the ones who asked all the nice girls.

The Spaz? I never went, of course. Never even occurred to me. I could have shown up in my too small grey flannel suit, but I knew it would have been pathetic.

They weren't girls, they were women, so confident, so lovely, so impressive, and what was I?

An Airfix modeller.

A Spaz.

That was June, and it was a funny thing, I decided I'd had a gutsful. No more bloody Spaz, no more being despised. I was going to do something about it.

So I did.

Pretty much as soon as school broke up, I decided

to lose some weight. I started to go cycling and running every day.

Now this was not easy. I'd spent so many years hearing abuse hurled at me by some arsehole teacher every time I was sent on a cross-country run. I could waddle 100 yards and then I needed to walk.

It was much the same when I tried now. A hundred yards the first day, two hundred the second. But inside a month I could manage a mile, and after another month it was two miles. No idea if I'd finally reached puberty, but the weight dropped off and I started to grow a muscle or two. In fact I started to grow in general. The stumpy Spaz was up to five foot nine by the time he joined the upper sixth, and was wearing normal sized trousers.

Not many people seemed to notice, but I didn't care. I was happier with myself and didn't seem to give a shit about looking brighter than the sportsboys. I wasn't so embarrassed about my piano lessons either, since I'd started to notice that being musical was quite attractive to some girls. No, of course, not the busty ones with the long blonde hair, they were still magnetically attracted to the rugby team. But some of the lesser ones, the fat girls, or the flat-chested ones with the big glasses started to seem interested. They were on my level, and, let's face it, they were all that I deserved...at the time.

I kept at the exercise, gave up on the fattier parts of my mother's cookery and most of the school stodge. By the time I came to sit my A levels I was as fit as anyone in the form, I was a shit-hot pianist and I was about to score three As. Rugby, my arse.

The last June of school, I was all set to leave, had university offers from Cambridge and London, had a reasonable dull flat-chested girlfriend called Margaret,(funny, rubbish girlfriends always seemed to be called Margaret) and things were going pretty well.

And nobody had called me Spaz for a whole year.

People had started to look up to me, the sports boys had been coming for some help with their English essays, some of the skiffle fans needed help with their chords and I was beginning to feel important. That Margaret girl was beginning to enjoy the fact that I wasn't the fat slob anymore and there was a virginity losing thing for both of us. From what I know now she wasn't much, but I doubt she's had better since. Call me arrogant.

That was school over with and it was time for university. I wasn't going to be stupid, I'd decided to make a fresh start. There was going to be no more Quentin Stanley Passmore. I was entitled to change my name to anything I wanted, so I did the deed poll thing, and it was Steve Moore who turned up in September at Cambridge University to read chemistry.

Well, my dear, let me tell you about the Saundersfoot Suicide case, as it wasn't called at the time. One of my more baffling cases from the days in South Wales. Or West Wales in this case, I suppose. Very interesting indeed, though I can't really claim that it was my finest hour as a detective, since it wasn't me who solved it. No bugger solved it really. In fact I'm probably the last one left alive who even knows there was a case. Hope the *Telegraph*'s going to end up printing this, I wasted a lot of time on those buggers at the *Mail*.

Well, perhaps I will have one just to loosen my tongue. Large gin and tonic if you would, my dear.

What?

Oh, alright, suit yourself, love.

Oh no better? Well, you'll have to excuse an old man *Otres tantes, otres moors* as the Froggies say.

Alright, Miss Tomkins it is.

OK then Mz, my love, whatever you want.

Ah, that'll do nicely.

So, *reverend a noose mutton,* eh?

I'd been seconded to the Pembrokeshire Police for a few months. My transfer to the Met was imminent, but Pembrokeshire were a bit short-handed. Outbreak of mumps or something. Mumps, my de...er...Mz Tomkins. Nasty thing, swollen neck glands if you're a kid. Some rather more personal glands in the adult male of the species, which can be very painful indeed. They give them jabs against it now, but not back then. I'd had it when I was eight, so no worries.

Yes, jabs now, but back in the dark ages kids used to catch the lot. Measles, Mumps, Chicken-pox, German Measles. I got them all when I was young. Except the German Measles, probably because Mother wouldn't allow anything German in the house. My Uncle Ken had a Heinkel bubble-car, but she wouldn't let him put it on the drive. He had to park it down the street when he visited, so she couldn't see it. Not one to forgive and forget was Mother, I think she was the only person I knew who missed rationing. She'd learnt her cookery in the days of powdered egg and Spam and it showed. I think they closed the Spam factories in mourning for a week when she died.

Sorry, wandering off again. Let's get back to Tenby.

Never been to Pembrokeshire? Lovely spot, plenty of beautiful coastline, pretty much unspoiled in those days, though I don't know about now. It's probably too far off the beaten track to have got all that commercialised, and I've no doubt it loses out to the cheap foreign holiday market.

Funny place mind you, that part of it from Carmarthen down to the coast. 'Little England Beyond Wales' they used to call it. Something to do with its having been settled by English people in the thirteen hundreds or something, I'm no historian. All around it was a stronghold of the Welsh language, but as soon as you got into South Pembrokeshire it was like crossing a line, and you'd only hear English spoken. Just as well for me, as I'd never picked up much Welsh at school. What little I ever did know is forgotten now, except maybe a few curses, and there's no call for those in Eastbourne. Though they probably don't count as curses now, the language you hear the young girls use to their kids.

So, anyway, Tenby Nick was my base for a while and I was lodging with a Mrs Arkwright in Sandy Hill over in Saundersfoot. Lovely little village that was. All built on steep hills running down to a beautiful sandy beach by the sea. Well, yes, I suppose all beaches tend to be by the sea, I'll leave you to sort out the grammar.

Nothing of it really, couple of banks and a Post Office, some little shops, mostly for holidaymakers, church, hotel, a few pubs, houses and plenty of guest houses. Still had a working harbour then for the fishermen to brink in their catches, and since we hadn't given away all our fish to the bloody Spanish, they could actually make a living at it. Long before the EU or whatever it's called this week. That was in the days when old President De Gaulle was still saying 'Non' every time we tried to join his Common market. Be a bloody sight better if he was still around saying it, if you ask me.

Tenby was just up the road from Saundersfoot, an oldish town, still with some of its wall intact. Another decent beach, a bit bigger. Very popular with the miners and 'Grockles' for their holidays at the time.

It was a bit of a holiday for me too really. Tenby was hardly the crime capital of Wales, so there was nothing much to do.

Until that Thursday.

I remember it was a Thursday, because a Test Match had started up at Lords. The West Indies I think, and I was trying to get a decent enough picture on the Nick telly to follow it. You won't remember the old black and white tellies and what a fuss it was to get a picture. They used to come with buttons on the back. 'Vertical Hold' and 'Horizontal Hold' and you had to fiddle about with them until the flashing lines stopped. Then you'd go and sit down and the bloody thing would start flickering again. So then you'd have a go at the aerial, see if that would do any good, and you'd probably find the best picture was with Grandad standing on the sofa and holding the thing halfway out the window. Not that my Grandad was in Tenby Nick that day. Or anywhere else since 1953.

What? Pushed for time? I daresay you've got a damned sight more time left to you than I have, young lady.

Alright, I'll get on with it.

It surprised my mother that I chose Chemistry, since I'd always been so good at English, but I had my reasons. I worked like a black the whole three years and took a first. Of course there'd been girls, quite a few of them, but I didn't let myself get distracted by them, I had work to do. Well, not all work, of course, I kept up the exercise, and improved my cricket out of all recognition. I narrowly missed my 'Blue' in the first year, but got it the next two. Third year was best, took 4-33 to help bowl out Oxford on the last day. No more Spaz for me.

It was a whole new life, but I hadn't forgotten the old one. And some of the people who'd contributed to it. One in particular I could still see, vicious swine that he was. Face always twisted in contempt, though of course I only saw it when he was looking my way. Big sod he was, though I'd expect he'd run to fat later. I'd be finding out anyway. Him and that girl who was always hanging on to his arm. She'd been lovely to look at, all tits and long blonde hair. Just as twisted inside as he was, mind you. She was the only girl who called me 'Spaz', the rest mostly had ignored me, but not her. Maybe she did it to impress him, but there was no need, he was besotted, the bastard. I could still hear them laughing at me. There's an old saying about people who laugh last, and they'd be finding out about that soon enough.

So, Stephen Moore left Cambridge with a First in Chemistry, but it wasn't time to use it just yet.

We got a call. Two deaths down in Church Street. Detective Sergeant Watson and I went down there to see who'd died in suspicious circumstances. Decent enough bloke Steve Watson, efficient and very quiet. Took a bit of ribbing about the name, they called him 'The Doc'. Very subtle and inventive people, policemen. Died a few years ago, I'm told.

Well, of course it was suspicious circumstances. No, the case, not DS Watson, he died of a stroke. Anyway, suspicious, the CID weren't generally called out when someone fell down the stairs, had a stroke or a heart attack. Two uniformed coppers had got there first and radioed for us.

No, I can't remember what sort of car it was, my dear, probably a Ford Zodiac since I was a Detective Inspector at the time. The Anglias were the Panda Cars in those days, from what I remember, and the Squad Cars were Zodiacs or Vauxhall Victors. It's a bloody long time ago as I say. No, never had Jaguars, they were just for the villains...in South Wales anyway. Or Inspector Bloody Morse, but he never worked down in South Wales. We'd have kicked him out soon enough, useless bad-tempered old sod. The guilty party is generally the only bugger he hasn't arrested at the end of the show.

Where were we? Ah yes, the murder, DS Watson and I were called out to the scene. Down to Church Street in Saundersfoot, as I said. Nice big house, so someone was doing pretty well for themselves. Dunno if it's still there, probably a small hotel now if it is. There was money about for sure, since there was a Jaguar on the drive, not that it really meant they were villains. Plenty of honest people drive Jaguars, or so I'm told.

Apparently it was the char who'd reported it. I was for arresting her straight away, since it always seemed to be chars who found bodies. Them and bloody dog walkers. Well, yes, and joggers too now, but you wouldn't have found too many joggers in Saundersfoot back then. Hadn't been invented, people just got old and fat without feeling guilty about it.

Char? The cleaning woman, Mz T, the lady who came in 'to oblige' as they used to say, on Tuesdays and Thursdays. I thought she'd keep for a bit and I got one of the constables to sit with her in the kitchen and give her a cup of tea, while the other one took me into the lounge to see the star attractions. Terence Bowen and his wife Valerie, according to the constable. Sitting comfortably on their smart red sofa. Both stone dead, or so it appeared to the untrained eye.

And to the trained eye too, since the police doctor had got there before us. Nobody was dead until he said they were dead. Except this time he was a she. Apparently the normal bloke was on holiday, so there was a locum woman there to declare them dead. Nice looking woman, though I don't remember her name. Little bit older than me, efficient and nice legs. Sorry, just put 'efficient' then.

Dead they surely were, but she had no idea why.

"If there were just one body, Inspector, I'd have said a heart attack. Trouble is you don't usually find two people having simultaneous heart attacks. Especially not in their forties. Something else, Iwould think. Probably poison, but you'll be needing a post-mortem.

For sure, life was extinct and had been for about twelve hours according to her. Stopped me arresting the char anyway. We sent for an ambulance to take the bodies off to Milford Haven hospital, but we had about half an hour before it would show up, so it was time to do some detecting.

Of course we were back in the stone age then, none of this climbing into paper suits and gumboots, swabbing everything in sight for that DMA stuff. Best we could manage was to dust for fingerprints, if any, and look around for those elusive clues you read so much about.

Let's see if the Williams memory is up to describing the scene for you. As I said, the two of them were sitting back on the sofa. Nice big red one, and there were two matching armchairs which didn't have dead bodies in. He was a biggish bloke, looked like a rugby player just starting to lose the battle with the beer. She was a good-looking woman, blonde, well-covered, probably very fanciable twelve hours ago, but now a bit dead for my tastes. Always was picky about that.

Joke, my dear. Actually I was courting at the time. Smart young WPC from Barry Nick. Jane Langdon. Lovely girl.

The deceased weren't dressed to go out. He was in trousers, shirt and cardigan and she had a patterned dress on. Looked a cut above catalogue to me, but I'm no expert in *hoot cutear*. Couldn't see any marks on either of them, so 'no signs of violence apparent' was written in DS Watson's notebook. Room very tidy, no signs of a struggle.

Looked for all the world as if they'd been having a nightcap, since there were two glasses on the coffee table in front of them, with a little clear liquid in each. I took a cautious sniff and they both gave off a whiff of gin, but I bloody well wasn't going to take a sip to make sure. The drinks would have come from the cocktail cabinet on the other side of the lounge, which seemed to be fairly well stocked with the usual spirits, some tonic water, a soda siphon. All the stuff you'd expect.

By now, the rest of the team had arrived to start bagging up anything useful and dusting for prints on glasses, bottles, doorknobs and anything else that looked hopeful.

I made a cautious search of the deceased.

Nothing to report from her. The dress had no pockets, and I wasn't about to inspect her lingerings. He was a little more helpful, since his cardigan had a pocket on each side. Nothing in his left one, but an empty brown medicine bottle in his right one. I took it out very carefully with a handkerchief. No label.

Well, I probably didn't shout "Aha!" but it seemed to be in the nature of a clue to say the least, so it was promptly bagged and sent off to be inspected by the Forensic people. I didn't open it, much less sniff it. Never sample anything you find at a potential crime scene, you'll live a lot longer that way.

We did a few more Detective-type things. The TV was built into a smart wooden cabinet opposite the sofa, and the doors were shut. I put my hand on it, but it was stone cold, so probably hadn't been used since the previous night. There were no signs of forced entry, no helpful size-twelve hobnail boot prints anywhere and nothing in any of the ashtrays for me to instantly deduce that the murderer had smoked Embassies and had pink lipstick. There were photos on the sideboard, taken at dinners, or so I suspected from the monkey suit and her dress. One or two of him in a rugby blazer, and the normal wedding photo from about twenty years ago at a guess.

Ah well, it was time to ask some questions.

Yes, the char. I thought it best to talk to her in the kitchen, rather than try to get comfortable in the living-room with two dead bodies looking at us. I asked the questions and Watson did the notebook bit. A good lad on the notebook, Watson.

Mrs Edna Perkins was the lady's name. I was never much of a description expert and it's nearly fifty years ago, but she looked like a normal woman in her late fifties. Fifty-seven I think it was. Not the preened up type you see these days, with all that

Bollox in their faces and silicon tits...pardon my *fransay.* She looked everyday of her age and maybe a few more. Dressed in an overall and the traditional lumpy headscarf.

No?

I suppose you don't see it so much now. Bit like that Hilda Ogden on 'Coronation Street'. They'd put all the rollers in their hair, spray it with some stuff or other and then spend all day with the headscarf on top. Sometimes even a net thing which really looked horrible. Come the evening, they were all ready to take the curlers out and look glamorous, on the off-chance that Cary Grant dropped over to take them down the Saundersfoot Hilton for dinner. Or, more realistically, ready to shove off down the bingo with some other old trouts.

Yes, all right, senior ladies if you prefer. Fifty-seven barely counts as old these days. Now she'd be down the gym at her Pirates class or whatever they call it, face lift, arse lift, tit-lift, but then people just got old without a struggle.

That was Mrs Perkins and you probably wouldn't have picked her out from all the other old dears in lumpy headscarves down the market or in the cafés. She smoked a lot, and the kitchen soon looked and smelled like a saloon bar with it. Maybe it was nerves, maybe she always did, I didn't ask. She wasn't as important as her story, of course.

Tuesdays and Thursdays were her days to 'do' the Bowens, though she 'obliged' another couple of people on different days. She'd arrived around ten-thirty, let herself in with her key, taken off her coat and gone straight into the kitchen, put on her gloves and filled a bowl with soapy water to get started on some washing-up. Not that Mrs Bowen ever left the evening-meal stuff for her, but there were usually one or two plates and the glasses from their nightcap gin.

"Oh yes, too right, they liked their nightcap, sir. Though she usually left the glasses by the side of the sink. Not this morning, that's why I went into the front room to look. That's when I found them. I knew they were dead with one look. Used to be a nurse in the war."

Now, of course, at this point, Mrs Perkins should have screamed blue murder, run into the road, roused the neighbours and caused a first-rate commotion, as in all the best crime novels. She didn't. Maybe as a nurse, she'd seen enough dead bodies not to panic, so she'd simply gone out the front door and dialled 999 from the phone box opposite.

"But there's a telephone in the hall, Mrs Perkins."

"Oh no, in the books the police always say, you mustn't touch anything, sir. I thought it best to go outside."

"Which books might they be?"

"Oh, I do love the Christies, and that John Creasey and Nagayo Marsh. I do get them from the library. I love a nice murder…oh, I didn't mean…"

No, of course not. I asked all the usual stuff, but she wasn't much help. She had her own key because the Bowens were never normally in when she came.

"In fact, I never seen him at all."

"So how do you know it is Mr Bowen?"

Aha, sharp detective I was.

"Well, I suppose I don't for sure. But he does look awful like all those photos in the front room."

Apart from that, she was a mine of no information. She didn't know what job either of them did, she supposed there were no children, she had no idea how well they got on, and no idea at all about how they came to be dead. Dreadful shock it had been, them sitting there like that.

We didn't keep her long after that and she went home in a police car. Can't remember where she lived. I think the neighbour opposite remembered her showing up at about the time she'd told us. Best to check everything. Always best to cross the 'i's and dot the 't's.

Now it was time to find out about the deceased.

I suppose you don't want chapter and verse of every enquiry we made, every neighbour we interviewed, the search for relatives and all that stuff? It would probably bore the ...er...bottom off your readers, and to be honest, it wasn't that exciting for us.

I'll cut it as short as I can.

As I said before, they were the Bowens. Terence Peter and Valerie Jane (née Hughes). He was manager of a branch of a national building society in Tenby and she ran a little arts and crafts gift shop in Saundersfoot. He was a pillar of the local rugby club, though he'd stopped playing a couple of years before. Just beginning to transfer his allegiance to golf, it seemed, and she was quite a keen member of the Ladies' Section.

Ladies' Section of the Golf Club, love. They weren't allowed to be full members. I think they even had to use a separate entrance and weren't allowed in the main bar unescorted.

Yes, shameful indeed, but you must remember that women had only been given the vote a year or two before, so it wasn't surprising. All changed now, I'm sure.

I quite agree, dreadful chauvination. Yes,no doubt pastariarchal nonsense too, but let's get back to the Bowens. shall we?

First thing we needed was someone to identify the *corpuses delictusees*, which proved a little more difficult than it might have been, since both sets of parents were dead. It's not really all that long ago, but most people in those days didn't manage much more than their three score and ten. Seventy, Mz T, it's what the Bible promises us, though some of us get a little bonus. In the end I believe it was a brother who did the necessary, though I don't remember whether it was his or hers. So, identified they were, and then the post-mortem could get under way.

Not that we'd stopped asking questions, of course. Neighbours, friends from the Rugby and Golf Clubs, people at the building society, the few relatives we managed to turn up. Usual sort of thing. Any signs of trouble in the marriage? Any financial worries? All pretty routine, since we had no idea what we were dealing with until after the post mortem and the forensic stuff.

The post-mortem came through first. Surprise, surprise...they hadn't had simultaneous heart attacks after all.

They'd been poisoned.

Some sort of alkaloid vegetable or vegetable alkaloid thing, though the exact stuff would take a while to pinpoint. More laboratory stuff. Things moved a lot slower in those days. Whatever it was it was pretty fast-acting, probably tasteless and odourless. The pathologist's guess was nicotine.

Yes, love. The stuff they put in fags to get you hooked on them, and in those little patches that are meant to unhook you. Apparently if you take all the nicotine from a packet of twenty and swill it down, you'd drop dead straight away. No, no, I doubt that they'd done clever stuff with packets of Players, nicotine was quite common for spraying roses back then. Kill the greenfly, or what have you. Smoker are you? Well, enjoy it while you may, they're your lungs. Never could stand it, myself.

No, poisons weren't hard to come by back in the dark ages. Most garden sheds might have nicotine, some cyanide for killing wasps, arsenic or strychnine for rats and mice and God knows what all else. If you've ever read any Christies you'll know that irritating people never lived too long for want of some handy poison. Sometimes I wonder how most husbands survived.

Well, no...fair play, Mr Bowen didn't and nor did his wife.

Pretty soon the pathologist's guess was proved right by the labs. Nicotine it was. The scene of the crime boys probably used the same lab, because their results came back at the same time. Or mostly lack of results, since there was no trace of anything nasty in any of the bottles of spirits or the mixers. I even got them to test the ice-trays in the fridge, which I thought was quite clever of me, but they were just water. Nicotine wouldn't have frozen anyway, apparently.

But they did find some nicotine. In both the glasses from the coffee table there were traces, and in the brown bottle in Bowen's pocket.

Food for thought indeed, and at least we had some direction to go in with the questioning now. Did they have any enemies (well, who did in Saundersfoot, but we always had to ask). Back again to poking our noses into the marriage, but there was no talk of affairs or any other problems. Their finances seemed fine, it was a big house they had, but they'd paid the mortgage off years before after inheriting from the parents, both sets of whom had not been short of a few bob. We talked to the local quack, but he had nothing useful to add, he hadn't seen either of them for years, not since Bowen had broken his arm playing rugby.

There was no note left by either of them, not that suicides always do, so nothing to go on there. No signs of a break-in, nothing seemed to be missing from the house, no signs of violence on either one. No strange fingerprints to be accounted for. Just theirs as it turned out, since Mrs Perkins always wore her rubber gloves to clean and seemed to do a good job of dusting and polishing. We spoke to some friends who'd been round for drinks the previous weekend, but their prints had all been cleaned off by the Thursday.

The only useful prints we were able to find were on the bottle. Bowen's.

So, we'd tried our best, but we had bugger all in the way of an explanation. All we were able to tell the *Tenby Echo* was that we weren't currently looking for anyone else in connection with the deaths.

After that it was up to the coroner and his jury. As far as I was concerned, Bowen had killed himself and murdered his wife, but there was always the possibility that she'd known and they'd had a suicide pact together. There was nobody to ask. In the end the local jury seemed to want to be considerate of everyone's feelings, and they brought in an open verdict on the two of them. Dodged the issue, if you ask me. Nobody did, mind you.

It went down in our files as a closed case.

Might well have stayed that way, if not for subsequent events.

Time for another? Large one for me, my dear.

Sorry, sorry.

I planned to train as a Pharmacist. A Chemistry degree is very useful, but it tends to concentrate on the theoretical. Pharmacy shows you the practical, the effects of drugs on the human body, how they combine, the different dosages that can produce effects, from the beneficial, to the harmful, to the fatal. I found it fascinating stuff. I kept thinking of people I'd like to test things on. That nasty pig Probert for one. Wasn't enough, just words with him. He was always trying to find new ways to bugger up my life, Right from the first year, when he'd tied my boot laces in such tight knots it took me twenty minutes to undo them and I got such a bollocking from the horrible rugby teacher. Even when he got older, he wouldn't stop. He put jam in my hair once, and then bent my flute. Just out of spite, I hadn't done anything. Cost ten pound to have it fixed, and I told my mother I'd dropped it.

"Poor little Spaz, his blowpipe's bust."

Yes, there were a few things off the shelves I'd like to stick in that bastard's beer.

But patience, eh. He could wait.

Ah, nice. Thank you. Here's to *The Telegraph*, eh? Grand paper it used to be, though gone like all the rest now, all TV stars and women's fashions. Always used to get it for the sports sections, but they've cut those right back. Anyway, best of health to all who sail in it. A drop or two always helps the memory. Though I find it easier to remember the sixties than I do last week. The number of times I go upstairs and forget what it was I wanted. Or I change tack halfway through a sentence, used to drive the wife mad.

The case. The Bowen suicides were closed as far as we were concerned. I'm trying to tell the story the way we learnt about it, see. Of course, I could just cut to the end and explain the whole thing if you think your readers would prefer it that way? I thought they might like the build-up, sort of thing. More tension and suspense that way isn't it. And I'm in no hurry if you aren't? Good.

Well, there wasn't a lot happening in Saundersfoot that summer for the police to get excited about. The Mods and Rockers weren't inclined to come out as far West as Wales, they generally stopped at Minehead, so the only trouble was the odd bit of argy-bargy between some local boys and the tourists after a few pints too many. That was generally sorted out with a few stern words from the constables, though there was the occasional night in the cells for one or two, perhaps even a fine the next day. None of the viciousness you see these days, mind you. People hadn't generally got into the habit of carrying a knife on a night out.

Not a great deal to interest a Detective Inspector at all, I fear. But there were plenty of other distractions. The West Indies were giving England a proper pasting at cricket and Sobers and his boys were a joy to watch. Course we never saw too many blacks in Wales in those days, so it was quite a big thing when they played Glamorgan at Swansea, and I took a day off to see some of the game.

What? The football? Well, yes, it was the World Cup that year, but it wasn't of all that much interest to us Welsh. Can't remember the Welsh football team ever qualifying for the finals, and probably the majority of Welshmen ended up cursing that boss-eyed Russian linesman. None of the games were played in Wales or Scotland, so it was a completely English party, and they could bloody well get on with it as far as we were concerned. Haven't they all been bleating on about it for forty years since, mind you.

No, sorry, I'm not really much of a Welsh Nationalist, I haven't lived there for the best part of four decades, so I'm not going to pretend to hate the English now, even if they are a bunch of bloody twisters.

Yes, yes, the case.

As I was saying, I'd been having quite an easy summer, enjoying some decent weather, trips down to Tenby beach and popping in to a dance or two here and there at weekends. Met one or two nice local girls, and even a holidaymaker or two who seemed quite friendly, once I learned to decipher the Birmingham accent. Not that anything ever came of it, of course. I did tell you I was courting, didn't I? Funny place Birmingham, did you know they've got more miles of canals than any other city in the world? Half the girls didn't know that either. More immigrants too, but I daresay you won't be wanting to print that.

Yes, I'm getting to it.

I remember that it was a Monday in July, not sure if it was before the World Cup Final or after now, long time ago, Mz T. Ten o'clock we got the call. Another suspicious death, down in Vicarage Lane.

In fact at the Vicarage.

By pure coincidence, the Vicar.

The Reverend Aneurin Probert. Church he was, not Chapel. Vicar of the parish of Tenby and Saundersfoot. Been there quite a few years, well-respected local man, highly thought of and never a whiff of scandal, despite not being married.

Dead now, his head in a gas oven apparently.

Well, of course, Watson and I went down to have a butcher's at the scene.

Nice big house, The Vicarage. When Watson and I rolled up there were two Panda cars on the drive and a blue Ford Cortina which I assumed to be the quack's car. She was in there along with some constables and had just declared life extinct. Not surprising really, since His Reverence was lying on the kitchen floor with his head inside the oven. Good job it wasn't electric, or he'd have been done to a turn.

No, I suppose it isn't funny. Most of my little jokes never were and they get no better with repetition.

Gassing yourself use to be quite popular for suicides in those days, since we mostly used the town gas which was poisonous. Now it's all North Sea gas, which is different stuff and won't poison you. It'll still suffocate you if you're really determined, but nowhere near as quick.

I got the outline of the story from Constable Davis. A good man, twenty years in. The housekeeper (who struck me as being almost as suspicious as a char) had turned up at eight, ready to cook the Reverend's breakfast, but had almost been knocked over by the stench of gas as soon as she came in the front door. She'd opened as many windows as she could, and then made for the kitchen with a scarf over her face. She'd taken one look and seen that the Reverend would be preaching no more sermons. Fair play, she'd had the presence of mind to turn the oven off and open all the kitchen windows before calling the police. I suppose she'd been quite lucky that she hadn't been smoking when she walked in. If she smoked.

That was something I could ask her afterwards, if I remembered. For the moment we had a routine to go through. The doctor thought that death was due to gas poisoning, which seemed to be a reasonable guess in the circumstances. Probably sometime around midnight the previous night. Bloody lucky that the gas hadn't caused an explosion, not that Reverend Probert would have noticed. Maybe one of the windows had been open a crack and let some of it out.

As I said, the Reverend Probert wasn't married and lived there alone. He had a housekeeper, but she didn't live in. She'd come over most days and cook his meals, keep the place clean. Sunday she didn't come, but that was his busy day, so he was happy to shift for himself. According to the housekeeper, he'd seemed perfectly normal and cheerful when she'd left him on the Saturday evening at about seven. Working on his sermon for the following day according to her.

Not sure that I do remember her name now...Thomas, Davies or Jones I suppose. She was in the hell of a state and it took a long time to get her statement. That's why I'm not trying to give it *verbosetim*, it would take forever. Essentially all she could tell us was that she'd found him as previously mentioned.

The fingerprint boys came and went. There weren't too many things to take prints off. All the dinner stuff was washed up, there were no convenient glasses about, but they did what they could, especially the cooker. I got them to do the door knocker and bell too, perhaps His Reverence had received a late caller. Not unusual for a vicar to receive his flock at all hours.

By now the Reverend Probert was on his way to the hospital and I was determined that he should have the most thorough post-mortem possible.

You see, I wasn't having this one as a suicide. It all seemed so unlikely.

I've seen my fair share of suicides over the years, many more since that one than before, and they generally follow some sort of pattern. First, there's usually a note, not always, but usually. Second, it's often not the first time they've tried, maybe a few cries for help before they do it seriously. And they fall into one of several groups. Teenagers, who don't realise that whatever seems so bloody devastating now would have been forgotten about in a few months. Older lonely people who've given up. People with big financial worries, and of course the mentally ill.

A group of people who almost never kill themselves are ministers of religion. In fact I'd never heard of one before, and I haven't come across one since. Like I said, I wasn't having it.

I didn't overlook anything. I ordered all the bottles in the drinks cabinet and all the food in the fridge to be taken away for analysis, we checked every door and window for signs of forced entry. We tried to get the housekeeper to check if anything seemed to be missing, which was none too easy, since she kept collapsing in tears. We interviewed all the neighbours, none of whom had seen any visitors calling at the Vicarage on Sunday night. Not that they would have been likely to, as the house was a big one, stood back from the road with a fair length drive leading up to it.

The whole house was thoroughly searched, which was probably fairly useless, since we had no idea what we were looking for. Everything in his medicine cabinet was taken away to be looked at.

Nothing.

Nothing at all to suggest anything other than what it appeared. Suicide by gas poisoning.

Same again. Wait for the post-mortem and nose around. Nosing around got us nowhere at all. The Reverend was well liked in the community, nobody had any idea why he might have topped himself. By all accounts, he'd been his usual cheerful self at Evensong which was pretty much the last time anyone could remember seeing him.

He was a local boy as it turned out, something of a rugby player too in his youth and at priest's college, or whatever they call it, but he'd given up once he qualified...what is it...ordained? He was still a regular spectator at Tenby's home games.

The snooping went on. He wasn't a rich man, but there were no money worries. As I might have mentioned, he was unmarried, but there was no whiff of scandal. No groping of the choir boys or midnight trysts with the organist. There seemed no reason at all why he'd suddenly decided to bid farewell to this cruel world. Unless there was some dreadful morbid depression that only affected exrugbymen.

Our only hope was the post-mortem.

That didn't help. Death was due to intoxication with town-gas. No signs of violence on the body, no dreadful wasting disease which might have led him to take an easy way out. The only thing that we hadn't known before was that he'd taken some barbiturates. Sleeping pills probably. Enough to make him very groggy, but not enough to cause death. Maybe some Dutch courage, was the quack's idea, especially as he'd also had a whisky or two. The vicar, not the quack.

We found a bottle in his cabinet, with a few sleeping tablets in. The medicine cabinet was otherwise completely devoid of any real medicine, just shaving stuff, spare soap and toothpaste. There was no doctor's or chemist's label on the tablet bottle, so we wondered where it'd come from.

I had a word with his doctor. Scotch bloke, McNab I think. Dunno what a Scotchman was doing in Tenby, but it wasn't illegal. Might be soon if they vote for independence. Good riddance, miserable tightfisted buggers.

Racist? How's that, the Jocks are the same race as the rest of us, just a bit paler and a bit less inclined to open their wallets. Ah well, cut it out if you think your readers will be offended, or outraged or whatever happens to *Telegraph* readers who read stuff they disagree with. I can't keep up with what's meant to be offensive from one month to the next. I swear they change it all every Michaelmas Tuesday just to confuse us all and take fresh offence.

Anyway, back to the Scotch quack.

"Definitely not, Inspector. The Reverend was in very good health, and I think I only ever saw him a couple of times. A mild eye infection and a sprained ankle, I seem to remember. He never mentioned any difficulty sleeping, and I'd probably have suggested a wee nightcap rather than pills anyway."

I assumed that a 'wee nightcap' wouldn't have meant a glass of piss before retiring. Bloody funny language, Scotch.

So, the mystery deepened. I suppose he could have scrounged some pills from somebody, but no-one owned up to that.

It was the same as the Bowens. Couldn't have been anything else but suicide, no sign of anyone else involved, but no reason at all that we could find why he should suddenly take it into his head to top himself.

Suicide it was though, and we pretty soon had the coroner's word for it. There really wasn't enough doubt for the jury to go for an open verdict, no matter how much they wanted to spare his parents' feelings. This one made the national papers since it wasn't every day that a parson was found with his head in an oven.

I had a long talk with the Tenby Superintendent

about it. Decent bloke Jeff Jones was, none of that anemonosity they always have to shove into the crime books these days. Compulsory isn't it, the desk-bound pedant and the maverick DI, always at each others throats. I gave up reading crime books when Agatha Christie died, just a succession of bloody clitches now. The Scotch ones are the bloody worst. Serial killers, drunk policemen and bloody rain. Not that we didn't get plenty of rain in Wales, mind you. And drunk policemen too, come to that.

Where did I get to? Oh yes, talking to the Super.

"It doesn't feel right, sir. The Bowens made no sense to me, and now this one makes even less. There's just no bloody reason for it."

"Not everything has to make sense, Williams and there's nothing to go on. No connection that you could find between the two cases, was there?"

"None at all. The Bowen's weren't church-goers, they may have known Reverend Probert through rugby or something else, but there's nothing to suggest they were close friends. The cause of death was different in both cases. The only similarities are the lack of note and the lack of any obvious reason."

"Well, it's not enough to start looking for a serial murderer, is it?"

"No, I suppose not. But it just doesn't feel right."

"Aye, I agree with you. And I've got a great deal of

confidence in a copper's nose. If something doesn't smell right, it often isn't. Keep half an eye on it, Williams. Who knows when something new might turn up?"

It was as far as he could go, of course. We couldn't ignore the two verdicts from coroner's juries, and there seemed not a clue to anything other than suicide. I'm not sure we even use the phrase "serial murderer" back then, since they pretty much never existed. Still don't except in those bloody books. There certainly was no such thing as serial suicide.

Wait and see seemed the only option.

Yes, of course in the books and films this is where we'd have called in the gifted amateur to sort it out for us. Sadly there is no such, MzT. No fat Frenchy with his green cells, no bloke in a deerstalker telling me that, once I'd eliminated the impossible, whatever remained and all that. Not even some old biddy from the village to look over her knitting and tell me how it was just the same as when the Corona popman ran off with the butcher's boy or whatever. .

Not that I decry the books, I'm a big fan of most of them. Come in all shapes and sizes, don't they...blind ones, fat ones, cripples, Chinks.....er sorry Chinamen....no? Chinese people? I like that 'Monk' myself...you seen him? He's got that Obstetric Consumption Disorder, so everything is a phobia for him. Brilliant.

But the only problem with people like that is they

don't exist. Here on Planet Earth we can't shout for help, so it's the poor policemen who have to do the detecting. Imagine the stories if they were just about Inspector Lestrade, Chief Inspector Japp, Inspector Cramer, Captain Stottlemeyer or Detective Inspector Williams. Not quite so glamorous then.

What I'm saying my dear, is that the buck stopped with us. If we couldn't solve it, nobody could.

I never did qualify as a pharmacist, but then it hadn't been my plan. There was a lot of criticism of me when I left to do my National Service, since I could easily have deferred it. But my father, my real father, had been in the forces and I was determined to follow him. Maybe somewhere he'd be looking down on me proudly. It was meant to be two years, but I made it plain from the start that I wanted to stay longer. I worked hard on all the basic training, turned out to be a very good shot and, after a year, I put in for a transfer to the Commandos.

I took to it like a duck to water, lapped up all the unarmed combat stuff and learned lots of nasty ways to kill people without making a sound. Of course, we weren't at war, but I was sent on several missions out in Aden and even spent some time working with the Americans in Korea. I killed people too, but we can't go into that, it's all Military secrets.

It soon became none of my business. The mumps thing seemed to disappear with the warm weather, leaving several officers less confident in their stones than they had been, and I was no longer required in Tenby. Didn't go back to Barry Nick straight away, since I was due my summer holidays.

By a fortunate coincidence, (which might have had something to do with bribery and corruption) it turned out that my holidays were the same two weeks as Detective Constable Jane Langdon, also of Barry Nick, and, after a glass of Babycham or five, she'd been persuaded to come away with me. Rather daring for those days, but she wasn't the sort to bother what other people thought. I don't remember whether I told my mother, I may have just said I was going away with friends. She could be a little old-fashioned could Mother, even by the standards of the sixties. Truth to tell, even by the standards of Queen Victoria.

Well, we'd decided that since it was our first trip away together, (PC Langdon, not mother, keep up!) we were going to push the boat out. No expense spared, the holiday of a lifetime to a dream destination.

A caravan in Porthcawl.

No? Well, I'm not surprised, it's hardly the place to attract sophisticated Londoners these days. But back then people weren't in the habit of jetting off abroad. For a start half of Europe was under military rule, so Greece, Portugal and Spain were out. And besides, aeroplane fares were a King's ransom, and if you did get as far as France, you could only take twenty quid out of the country with the exchange controls. Don't think I even owned a passport till I was thirty. So, everyone I knew holidayed in Wales.

Great place Porthcawl in the summer. The miners used to flock to the town for their holiday fortnight. Probably declined a lot since then, what with one thing and another. No miners for a start. No bloody mines left in Wales at all now. Bloody Scargill that was.

What? Well, you can blame Lady Thatcher if you want, God rest her soul, but she did more for this country that any of those union bastards ever did. Look at 'em, destroyed the mines, destroyed the car industry. I remember the three day week and the power cuts, young lady, rubbish piled up in the streets and nobody able to get to work. If it weren't for Maggie, we'd be living in a third world country now. Mind you, the state of London these days...

Ah well, I'm wandering off the point again. You're entitled to an opinion, though you might have a different opinion if you'd been alive at the time.

So, the pleasures of the Welsh Riviera it was. And pleasure it certainly proved to be, Mz T. Two weeks of sun, sea, sand and ....er....one or two other things. It was a good time for all that sort of thing. The girls were just starting to discover the Pill, which meant they could be a little more free with their favours than before, and we didn't have to worry about those.... whaddatheycallums... condiments. We used different words for the bloody things. Never got on with them. Used to sell them in the barbers for some reason. 'Anything for the weekend, sir?' they'd ask. Course, in those days my dear, sex was illegal from Monday to Thursday. Anyway, I never used the things, bloody horrible and slimy.

Safe sex? Bless you my dear, it wasn't dangerous. Not unless you called her by the wrong name halfway through.

Yes, she was an enthusiastic young madam in those days. Looked a damned sight better in a bikini than a police uniform too, I can tell you. Proper Welsh colouring, dark hair and green eyes. Nice baps in those days too. Happy days, the pubs along the promenade, fish and chips, cooking breakfast together on the Calor-gas stove, not that I helped much, maybe just kept her baps out of the fat. I wasn't much of a fan of the chemical toilet, I must say, especially emptying it, but it was only a minor drawback. I suppose things are a bit less primitive now.

We loved the funfair at Sandy Beach, though I showed my grandson some photos and he said it was 'lame'. I suppose the big dipper doesn't look too big if you've been to Disneyland, but it used to get the girls screaming and ready to sail on the boats through the 'Tunnel of Love'. Jane's favourite was the dodgem cars, and I used to tell her she drove the same way in a police car. Mistake that, she had quite a strong right hook. Dunno if they still have the same things at fairs now…candy-floss, Mr Whippy, bloody toffee apples which probably finished off what few teeth the NHS dentist in Barry had left unscathed.

We had a couple of rainy days though, and we spent some time talking over the suicides. She was a smart enough girl, so she had an idea or two in a theoretical way, which might have been worth exploring if it was any of my business. We didn't spend all that much time on it, there were other ways to pass rainy days that seemed more interesting.

So, our first holiday together, and probably still the best one, for all that we've done most of the world over the years. We both came back brown and relaxed. The brown thing was unusual, since most people ended up red and peeling, but we were big suncream fans. Useful stuff, suncream...amongst other things, it protects you against sunburn, if...er...properly rubbed in. God, it was a long time ago, but bloody happy days.

Poor old Jane.

The time flew past, and we were soon heading back to Barry. She was back to work on the Monday, but I had a few more days of leave stored up. It was pretty much the end of the summer. Welsh summers don't last long, and it rained for a few days, so I was at a loose end.

I decided to amuse myself with taking another look at the Saundersfoot Suicides.

Unofficially of course.

Now these days if you want to find out anything you switch on the computer and use Joogle. If you're a policeman, then you use the National Police Computer which will tell you pretty much all you need to know about everything and everybody.

No such luck in 1966. A computer was generally the size of a huge room with spools of tape going round and lights flashing on and off. The only place you were likely to find one was on *Dr Who* or *Thunderbirds* and they weren't going to help me. So the only option back than was the policeman's true friend.

Legwork.

Now all detectives have their little ideas about how to investigate. Holmes was a man for observation and detail, Poirot, he took the psychological approach. Me, I always looked at motive first of all, and my usual starting point was that *cooeey bonio* thing. That's Latin, Ms Z. It means "who cops for the loot?". Follow the money.

So I did, or tried to.

I drove over to Pembrokeshire, long before motorways so took me a while. Vauxhall Viva I had. I never liked driving, but I could hardly get a police driver. I saw the Bowens' solicitor, Mr Herbert, I think it was. Should have spoken to him before maybe, but we'd been short handed back in June, and it hadn't seemed all that important since we weren't required to investigate much.

It was a bit of a mess apparently, since neither of the Bowens had thought to make a will. Well, youngish people rarely do. And also there was no way of knowing which of them had died first, which could have made quite a difference to the inheritance line. Fortunately there were only two interested parties, his brother and her sister, or *vicky versa,* and they'd made no objection to taking half each of whatever the government had left. Quite a substantial sum for those days.

The brother apparently ran a string of garages and car showrooms around Milford Haven and was reputed to be rolling in money. The sister was married to quite a prominent solicitor in Cardiff, and was also not short of a bob or two. What the Bowens had left was certainly not chicken feed, and I've known murder done for an awful lot less, but it seemed unlikely that either family member had popped round and forced them to drink neat nicotine. I had no call and no permission to go bothering the brother and sister with yet more questions, they'd already been interviewed and shed no light on anything.

I tried His Reverence next.

He had made a will as it turned out, and it was very simple indeed. Half of everything he possessed went to his parents, and the other half to the Church In Wales. Not that he possessed much, country parsons rarely make the millionaire bracket. I doubted that it would have been sufficient to persuade his parents to kill their only son, nor for a team of cash-strapped Bishops to descend on the Vicarage and slaughter him.

As I said before, I've known murder done for an awful lot less, but I just couldn't see it happening.

Dead ends again, my love.

That was pretty much all I could do, since I wasn't officially on the case. I believe I called up Steve Watson and we sank a few beers and talked things over. He had no more ideas than I did, and probably less interest. Coroner and his Super had said suicide, so that was good enough for him. I ended up staying the night in his spare room. since I didn't fancy three hours in a car at night, drunk.

Not that I was the typical alkie DI, but I did like a few beers. I was just beginning to put my own rugby days behind me, so I had to watch it, didn't want to get fat. Yes, I suppose it is a lost cause these days, but back then I had young ladies to impress. Well, make that 'young lady' will you? Though there's very little chance of Mrs Williams ever reading it, even if the *Telegraph* sees fit to print it.

That do you for today? Same time next week, then?

After three years I was a captain in the Commandos, but that's when I handed in my resignation. They tried to talk me out of it, told me I could be a Colonel in another two years, but I'd learnt enough in the army, and I had work to do.

Women, oh yes, I'd met quite a few during my army days, usually sisters or friends of other officers when I was on leave and they invited me out to their houses. I was always very popular with other officers. Nice girls they were too, but I wasn't ready to settle down and I didn't want to treat them badly.

Not like that pig Hopkins at school. He'd have a new one every month, often two or three on the go at the same time. There were rumours he'd got the French mistress in the family way, but most people didn't believe that and said she'd just gone back to France. He was always talking about the girls behind their backs, very disrespectful. He still had time to take the rise out of me.

'So, Spaz, you courting yet? Or is Jane Russell a bit busy this week? Why don't you ask Alun if he'll lend you a nice sheep, eh? No, you wouldn't know which end of your dick to use would you?'

Found himself very funny did Hopkins, always. Maybe he'd be laughing on the other side of his face pretty soon.

Hello young man, what happened to Mz T then? Oh well, yes, I suppose an interview with Justine Beeber is much more important than an old fart like me. Who is she? Oh, begging his pardon. I don't keep up with rock and roll music. Dare say we'll cope without Mz T, one of those Women's Lib types, wouldn't surprise me if she burns her bra at weekends.

Oh, sorry about that. When's the wedding?

Yes, well...each to their own.

Let me see if I can remember where we'd got to with her? Perhaps a drink might help me to think. Nice, large gin and a splash of tonic. And have one yourself, tell them to put it on Superintendent Williams's slate. We can drink to your future health and happiness.

Huh, rather him than me.

Thank you young man. Cheers, eh?

So anyway, I'd done my stint up round Tenby, had a great holiday and reported back for work at Barry Nick on the Monday morning. My transfer to the Met was pretty much done and dusted, so I was really just marking time and not likely to get put on any important cases. I seem to remember spending a day or two chasing up some funny business down at the Docks....don't remember what now, but that all came to an end on Wednesday lunchtime.

Good old Charlie Watkins called me into his office.

Apparently they'd had a request from Tenby CID to borrow me again, *toot sweet* as the Froggies say.

Yes, of course.

There'd been another one.

I was getting to know the coast road pretty well by then, Cardiff, Neath, Port Talbot, Swansea, Carmarthen, St Clairs and on up to Tenby. All changed now, I suppose. All the mines and heavy industry gone, and I'm bloody sure the roads are a lot better. Not that I had to worry about that, as a Detective Inspector I rated a police driver. By another of those happy coincidences I sometimes managed to engineer, it was WPC Langdon. And since there and back in one day was a little much, she put up at the Royal Castle for the night. I'm not at liberty to say if she had an escort at dinner, or any night time visitors.

Mind you, before all that, I'd checked in at Tenby Nick to see what all the fuss was about. And fuss there surely was young man.

Michael Charles Hopkins had been found dead in his fume filled garage that morning, slumped in the driver's seat of his Rover.

As the Super put it,

"The garage was full of enough fumes to kill a regiment. Engine must have been running all night, and it had just about run out of petrol by the time we got there. Called by a neighbour who saw the fumes coming out under the door. Just as well they didn't try to open the door, or we'd probably have had two corpses."

Well, I had a few questions before I set off for a look at the scene of the...er...demise. Apparently Mr Hopkins was divorced and lived alone. No char or housekeeper (there went another bloody theory). Certainly not short of money, ran a family firm of solicitors. No note again.

"So why the big fuss about another suicide? I know four in a couple of months is a bit unusual, but we'd decided there was nothing suspicious about the others."

"I suppose you don't know who Michael Bloody Hopkins was, Williams?"

"Rings no bells with me."

"Only the bloody Mayor of Tenby."

Oh bugger.

Obviously the deceased had been hauled away for the post mortem and it was getting late, so we decided that my looking at the house could wait till the following day. Mrs Arkwright's boarding house was full up, so it was a night for me at the Royal Castle, and maybe look for something cheaper the next day.

I passed a comfortable night. Very comfortable. Yes.

I was up with the lark (or maybe even FOR a lark, eh, young man?) the next day and off up to Manor Road to meet DS Watson and take a shufti. A look, young man, yes, I'm a bit out of date. Past my sell-by date too probably.

Lovely big house, but then you rarely find a poor lawyer or politician and this bugger, or ex-bugger, had been both of them. The garage was attached to the house, and apparently the house had been locked up tight front and back. It seemed he'd driven home, pulled into the garage, shut up the door and proceeded to top himself.

Tracing his movements the previous night had been easy enough. He'd been at some Town Hall reception for something or other. Apparently left around eleven, after quite a few drinks.

"According to most people there, he'd pretty much had a skinful," was the way DS Watson put it.

Breathalyser? Not a chance. For a start, I'm not sure they'd even been invented then, and the police certainly weren't out at all hours looking for drunks. Besides, what copper in his right mind was going to stop the Mayor and a local magistrate to boot?

No, it wasn't corruption, just a little turning of a judicious blind eye. Though, it would have been healthier for him if they had pulled him in and he'd spent a night in the cells. He'd have had a damned sight better chance of waking up in the morning.

Well, the scene of the crime boys had been over everything, and the car had been hauled away, so there wasn't that much to look at. The garage door had apparently not been locked, but then it couldn't be locked or unlocked from the inside. The key was on the same key ring as the car key, which had been found in the ignition, fairly obviously. The garage was a wooden affair, with two wooden doors. Rough wood isn't a great surface for prints, and they hadn't found anything of interest. The driver's side of the car was covered in his prints, the front and rear passengers' areas had plenty of smudges, but nothing that looked promising.

They'd been over the house, though it seemed he hadn't gone inside on the night in question. Nothing seemed out of place, though who could say, since he lived alone? Well, actually his cleaner could have said, but it wasn't her day, which was just as well for her or I might have arrested her just for fun. I don't remember her name, but when one of the others tracked her down, she had nothing useful to add.

So, if we were going to get anywhere, the clues would have to come from the body.

Which, sadly they didn't. The post mortem confirmed the obvious. Death from carbon monoxide poisoning. It also confirmed that he had indeed had a skinful, probably enough to make him very unsteady on his pins and not your first choice to cadge a lift home with. He'd also had some pain killers, but that was no real mystery, there was a bottle in the glove compartment and another in his medicine cabinet. Prescribed by his doctor, as we found out later. Lumbago or sciatica, back problems anyway. Bit of bruising around the mouth, probably due to falling forward against the steering wheel when he conked out.

There was some idea that the whole thing might have been an accident. Perhaps he'd pulled into the garage, left the engine running, shut the door behind him, got into the car to turn off the engine and then passed out with all the drink. Not impossible, I suppose, but it didn't seem that likely.

In short, nothing useful and it got us nowhere.

Yes, I think Mz T was getting a bit bored with hearing about us getting nowhere. That's the trouble with real coppering. there's frequently weeks and months of no progress, before something turns up that puts us on the right path. If it ever does.

This one was beginning to look like a real stinker.

You see, with most murders, it's pretty obvious straight away who's done the thing. Husband, wife, boyfriend, lover, bloke found holding the bloodstained knife. With these ones, if they even were anything but suicide, there was nobody to pick on.

Same with Hopkins. As I said before, he was divorced and his wife had gone to live with her mother in Merthyr. She'd spent that night at the pictures with two friends. James Bond. We checked. We checked every bloody thing, that's why it took so long. Hopkins had a bit of a reputation as a ladies' man, but we couldn't come up with a regular girlfriend, and three very respectable people had seen him get into his car to drive home alone. No, he hadn't seemed depressed about anything, no, he had no money worries, no, he wasn't dying of cancer and no, he'd never attempted suicide before. People were not keen to speak ill of the dead back then, but I gathered the impression that he was a bit of a 'drunken rodni' as my Mam used to say about people she had no time for. Which was quite a high percentage of the human race.

Now, young man, I gave you all that in a couple of paragraphs, but gathering that information, or lack of bloody information, took a team of coppers the best part of a week. They don't put that in a two hour episode of "Frost", do they?

Once again, coroner said suicide. Case closed.

But the Super wasn't having it, and I wasn't having it.

"Williams, there's no bloody shape to this. It's plain daft. Do you know how many suicides we've had in the last three years round here? Practically bugger all. Now we've got four in three months, and all completely unexplained."

"But there's nothing to link them, Sir. The Bowens and His Reverence no doubt knew the Mayor, but they weren't close. There's no such thing as serial suicide."

Course, I wouldn't have been so sure these days, young man. The bloody kids on Bookface and Twatter end up talking themselves into all kinds of things to try and sort out a little fame for themselves. My grandson was showing me stuff the other night. You read about suicide clusters now, half a dozen kids in the same area topping themselves, and their friends leaving tributes, 'One more angel in heaven', 'You're a legend mate, we'll never forget you.' All bollocks of course, inside six months they're just a bunch of dead flowers and a soaking wet teddy-bear in some corner of the crem. But back then we were primitive, if people wanted to communicate they had to leave the house and see their real friends. And none of these people had appeared to be keen members of a Kamikaze club.

"But where does it leave us Sir? There's not a single sign of any of them being other than suicides. Odd suicides, unexpected suicides, but what else?"

"Williams, last month we talked about a copper's nose. We've both got pretty good ones, so does this smell right to you?"

Well, of course it didn't. I told him about the bit of sniffing around I'd done the week before and he just grunted.

"Look, Williams, I've been on to Dai Watkins and he's lending you to me until your transfer comes through. I want you on this. Something stinks, and I want to know what. Preferably before any more of Pembrokeshire's leading citizens decide to do themselves in. Alright?"

Well, of course I was keen, young man. I hadn't liked anything about these deaths and it certainly looked a bloody sight more interesting than trying to track down fag-smugglers at Barry Docks.

First I needed to get organised. A place to live would be a good plan. In the end I rented a caravan at one of the local parks. Not as impressive as the Porthcawl one, but a bloody sight cheaper. Though I was on expenses of course. Most mod cons, and it actually ran to a proper toilet. I'd had a gutsful of the chemical rubbish.

They gave me an office in the Nick. They couldn't run to a DS, which was a shame as Steve Watson would have been bloody useful, but they did spare me a PC. To be more accurate a WPC, or a WDC as I seem to recall. Let's see if I can remember the name....yes...Vanessa...no...Veronica Holt. Blonde girl, I seem to remember. No fool by all accounts, and attractive enough I suppose if your tastes ran to pretty, curvy blondes. The uniform wasn't flattering back then...no wait...she was a Detective

Constable, so she'd have been plain clothes, not that I remember her clothes all that well.

Anyway, an office and a two-man team. OK, yes, yes...a two-person team. All ready to crack the mystery of The Saundersfoot Suicides.

Well, yes, fair point, two of them had been in Tenby, but I just thought it would make a good title when you get round to featuring it. Up to you of course.

So, where to start? My idea of following the money hadn't got me anywhere, and a quick look at Hopkins' will didn't seem promising. Half of what he left was put into trust for the two children of his divorce and the rest was divided between his ex-wife to provide for them, and his mother. His mother was in an old people's home, and certainly hadn't sneaked out to gas her only son.

So we needed another route into the bloody thing. What linked those four people?

Nothing at all seemed to be the answer. We tried everything that might make sense and plenty that didn't. They didn't have a club, church, bank, insurance company or even a blood group in common. They didn't share a doctor, a solicitor, a gardener or even a milkman. They weren't taking any experimental new medicines, hadn't been on holiday to the same places, hadn't been to a hypnotism show, or abducted by aliens. They hadn't served on the same jury. They hadn't served in the same regiment (His Reverence and Mrs Bowen had never been in the forces). The only real link was that they were all much the same age.

Again, I'm giving you that in a sentence or two, but it was days of legwork. All useless. We were beginning to think we'd looked everywhere.

No, we didn't discount the old *ABC Murders* idea of hiding one death in amongst a bundle of them to distract us. Try as we might we couldn't find any motive for killing any one of the four, though I was beginning to think that perhaps they might all be diversions and that number five would be the real one. I certainly wasn't prepared to wait for number five.

I decided to work backwards and start with the latest one. Mayor Hopkins. He was the only one who'd left someone behind who might conceivably have a motive for assisting his demise. The ex-wife. It was time to take a trip to the flesh-pots of Merthyr, with the skilled driving assistance of DC Holt.

Ever been to Merthyr, young man? No, not much reason why you would. It was a pleasure I'd denied myself up till then. Typical Valleys shithole. Built on coal, but that's all gone now. There was still quite a bit around then, and the pits were the main employers. Miserable place, slate-clad houses with tin baths hanging on the back walls, and outside toilets. Maybe all modernised now, but I'll bet it's still a bloody miserable hole, and everyone's probably out of work these days too. Even the drive up there was miserable, I remember it was a typical Welsh summer's day, pissing with rain and cold too. Up from Tenby, via Carmarthen, Swansea, Neath, Aberdare and finally Merthyr. Took bloody hours, but then everything did in the sixties. Slow cars and even slower roads. No motorways then, not in South Wales anyway.

The former Mrs Hopkins was living back with her mother, as I said before. The house was pretty full, I suppose, with them and her two kids, but they were out at school when we called. It was a nice enough house, a terrace like a lot of them in Merthyr. Two down three up and a cellar. No bathroom and downstairs and out the back yard if you needed to go. Not many of those left, even in the Valleys I expect.

We were shown into the kitchen, which used to be where most of the activity of houses like that took place, eating, bathing, drinking endless tea, reading the *Daily Mirror*, complaining to the neighbours when they dropped round. The old woman made us tea and brought out some packet cakes too, while we chatted. I was the only non-smoker as usual, but people didn't use to worry so much about that. They hadn't invented passive smoking, so I suppose nobody ever died of it.

After the first cup of tea, I insisted on interviewing Mrs Hopkins in private, so her mother made the great concession of letting us use the front room.

No? It's a dead custom I suppose. People used to live in the kitchen, which was generally the biggest room in the house and dominated by a huge table, generally covered in oil-cloth. Bit like lino, son. If they had special guests, or maybe for Sunday tea, they'd use the front room, what we call the lounge now, though of course, since everyone keeps the telly there, we use it all the time now. Not many keep a room for best these days.

So, Mrs Hopkins. Attractive woman, though probably not as young as she was painted. Yes, plenty of make-up and lipstick, though she might have put that on for our benefit. Well-fed, but it had mostly settled in the right places. 'Blowsy' my mum might have said, though you don't hear that word anymore. You're probably too young to remember Elsie Tanner on Coronation Street, but Mair Hopkins was pretty much a blonde version. Bottle, as DC Holt told me afterwards, but then there weren't too many natural blondes in Wales then. Maybe not DC Holt either, though I didn't ask her.

I said something about how sorry I was for the news.

"Buggered if I am," was her reply to that. "Good riddance as far as I'm concerned. He was a swine of a man."

Well, a new slant on the grieving widow bit. I asked her if she knew of anyone who might bear a grudge against her husband.

"Me for a start, a bloody big grudge. And then probably half the husbands in Pembrokeshire and every woman he forgot to tell that he was married. Pig. He cold never keep his bloody trousers on."

So, the late Mayor Hopkins had been something of a philanthropist?

"Thought he was bloody Casanova he did. Anything in skirts and he was like a rat up a bloody drainpipe. Made a fool of me all over Tenby. I took him back twice, but the third time I buggered off. Divorced now I am. He had to pay too."

I asked about the co-respondent in the case. Yes, another old term I suppose. When someone sued for divorce on grounds of adultery, they generally named the other guilty party. Fun that could be, you used to get a little bloke following straying husbands round to hotels with a camera to get the evidence. All changed now, no need to prove fault, just that 'irreconsolable differences' thing after a few months and off to start again.

"Sheila Sherman her name was, though I could probably have picked any one of half a dozen. I hear she threw him out a few months after. Pig he was."

I asked if she knew of any reason why he might decide to make away with himself, and that seemed to stop the flow of vitriol.

"No. No, that was very strange. If some jealous husband had shot the bugger or some woman had run him over I wouldn't have been surprised, but I could never imagine suicide. He thought far too much of himself. Probably couldn't imagine how the world would manage without him. Swine."

She'd mentioned jealous husbands twice, so I pressed her for names.

"Oh, any bugger whose wife he'd been after I suppose. No, I never actually saw any trouble. He was a big bloke, so maybe that's why he got away with it."

Ah, violent then?

"He was a bit in his younger days, but mostly grew out of it. I had a few slaps off the bastard when I made too much fuss about his goings-on."

She hadn't informed the police, women didn't much in those days. Probably the local bobby wouldn't have done much anyway. We were less inclined to get involved in 'domestic incidents' then. No, I'm not proud of it, just telling you what it was like. I'd hope things are better now, but who knows?

We stayed another half-hour, but got nothing much out of her. She knew of nothing that would have induced him to top himself, but then she hadn't heard anything from him in quite a while. If he'd been murdered she might have been an outstanding suspect. The terms of the divorce had obliged him to make a will providing for her and the children so she'd done well out of it, and we'd seen the animosity she still bore. Trouble was she'd been eighty odd miles away, had no car and her presence at the cinema with two friends had definitely been checked. And, of course, Hopkins hadn't been murdered.

I tried her with the names of the other suicides, but she'd never heard of any of them.

"I'm not from Tenby, see. I was on holiday down there when I met him at a dance. He used to drive up here every weekend when we were courting and stay Saturday night at *The Picton.* I didn't move down there till after we got married. Sorriest bloody thing I ever did. Swine, he was."

I assumed she had no plans to attend the funeral.

"Only if I can dance on the bugger's grave."

Perhaps that business of *de mortars nisi bonus* hadn't caught on in Merthyr.

We drove back, and agreed that we'd have done better spending the day on the beach than wasting it driving there and back. Then again it was raining, and we'd at least managed a bearable lunch at a pub outside Neath. Valleys' *cuisine* was generally not too *haute* but it kept body and soul together. We chatted about this and that all the way to the coast, she was a Cardiff girl who'd been in the police two years now and had hopes of being Chief Constable of the Met, or, failing that, finding some bloke to marry and giving it up to have children.

Well, I suppose that'll have to do for today, young man, time I was toddling along. Will it be you again next week, or the young lady? Hah, you could always toss a coin for it, and I'll see the winner next time.

What did he say barman?

Cheeky young sweep.

Hello again, young lady. Mz T isn't it. We missed you last time, still I had a good chat to the boyfriend.

What?

'Significant mother'? Who the bloody hell's that when she's at home? Oh, 'other'...I see. Well. Not really...bit out of touch, it's a long well since I was courting, as you'd probably guess.

Anyroad, I think last time I'd just finished telling the young man about driving up to Merthyr to see Mrs Hopkins as was, not that she added much to the sum of our knowledge. No idea why he might have topped himself and she didn't have a good word for him. Well, I suppose 'bastard' seemed quite a good word for him, come to think of it.

Next day we played the same game all over again, though this time it was a little nearer at hand. Pembroke Dock as I recall to visit the bereaved parents of the Reverend Aneurin Probert.

I suppose you've never had the pleasure of Pembroke Dock either? By the sea it was, people found it convenient to have a Dock as near the sea as possible back then. Busy little place in the sixties, shipping coal in and out. I believe Old Man Probert was something in the Coal Board, probably coming up to retirement then. Nice house they lived in.

A description? After all these years? You going to put up wanted posters? They were an old couple, my dear..er..Mz Turnbull. They were probably sixtyish and looked it. People used to look their age in those days, used to have a bloody hard working life in Wales and it generally showed. Mind you, it might have been that losing their only son had aged them even more. Dunno, I never saw them before.

He did most of the talking, it seemed that even trotting out a sentence would have her in tears still. Broken her it had. I don't think either of them lived more than a couple of years after that, I remember someone sending me the obituaries from the local paper.

I never got used to asking bereaved people stupid questions, not in forty years, and I was quite new to it then, Same bloody rubbish.

"No, Inspector, Aneurin wouldn't have made enemies. He was a bit of a boy in his younger years, especially when he was knocking round with the rugby team at school. Tidy little outside-half he used to be, and he'd have a few pints of a night…er… once he reached eighteen of course. I know he had hopes of a Blue when he went up to Oxford, but all that changed in his first term. He found God. His mother was so proud."

His mother gave a nod and a sniff. I noticed that father hadn't included himself in the pride. Maybe the Blue would have been more his style.

"I think it was some girl he met up there, took him along to meetings and services and before we knew what was what, he'd changed from Land Economy to Divinity, given up the rugby and had his nose in the Bible the whole time. His College weren't too happy really, as I think they'd been expecting him to do them proud on the rugby field, but there wasn't much they could do."

Silly bugger. I'd have given my right arm for an Oxford Blue, well, not that I'd have had much chance of one without my right arm…hehehe.

What? No, no disrespect to the differently abled at all, just an expression. Well, yes, alright, maybe an 'inappropriate' expression. No, I haven't seen a differently-abled sports team lately, I'm sure they do very well, considering.

Well, considering they can't walk or whatever, I dunno. And I don't need you to tell me what bloody century it is, young lady.

Very well, I apologise for the inappropriate language. And the negative reference to the differently-abled…shall we get back to the grieving parents?

"No, Inspector, he never played another game after that. Said that God had called him to higher things, though he used to go and watch the odd game when he came home in the holidays. He finished his degree, then took Holy Orders and was posted down here. Only a little parish, but it was near home and a start. Or it would have been."

Mother sobbed some more, so he sent her out to make a fresh pot of tea, and I asked about problems in the parish. Anyone who might have born him a grudge.

"I never heard about anything like that. But why are you asking? They said he killed himself? You're not suggesting…"

No, of course I wasn't suggesting, but his death had seemed out of character, so we were exploring all the possibilities we could think of.

"I suppose so. No, I can't think of anyone who'd want to hurt Aneurin these days. Though if there was someone, that would make more sense than him killing himself. I mean, that was a mortal sin to him. 'God gives life and only God can take it away.' I'd heard him say that more than once. I'll never believe that Aneurin killed himself. We can only think that there must have been some accident with the gas."

I couldn't see too many ways that His Reverence could have accidentally shoved his head in the oven and turned it on, but there was no point in saying so. I took a step or two onto even more sensitive ground and asked about his will.

"Yes, we all made one a year or two back. We'd had Twm Jenkins round for Sunday tea and he'd been talking about it and the trouble people caused by not making one and then dying when they hadn't planned to. Probably just looking for business really, but we all talked about it and went to see him that week to get them done. No idea that we'd be needing Aneurin's before ours, of course."

He looked as if he was going to cry himself now, but his wife came back in with more tea and Bourbons, to take his mind off it.

"It was little enough he left, just a few hundred in savings and what's left of his Church Pension. Just enough to bury him."

I supposed that parsons didn't get rich.

"Well, if he'd lived long enough, he'd have had a tidy bit from us, this house and what I've got put by, plus what his grandparents left us."

An excellent motive for murder then, but for the parents, not the son. I tried a few more avenues, but they were all *cool-de-socks.* They'd never known him depressed about anything, no financial problems, had lost interest in girls after he'd found God, had no health problems. No reason at all why he should want to make away with himself.

Another day wasted, though I had another pleasant drive back with DC Holt. Talked about this and that. She was from Cardiff as I said, not too impressed with Tenby. Bit slow after the big city. Nice girl she was, very friendly. I remember accidentally putting my hand on her leg a couple of times when she was changing gear. Clumsy of me.

Sexual harassment? No, my dear. Hadn't been invented. Anyway, she didn't seem to mind it too much. The working day was pretty much over by the time we got back, so she dropped me at my spacious executive caravan and took the car back to the nick.

The caravan had a barely functioning telly, but you could just about make out the picture if you fiddled with the aerial and the knobs enough. Must have been a Friday, since I remember I was all set to wander down the chippy then put my feet up and watch 'Double Your Money'. Probably Harry Worth and Dicky Henderson afterwards and so to bed. Telly used to finish early. Yes, you could Joogle them if you really wanted to, but I doubt your readers will be interested in fifty year old TV shows, or fifty year old suicides, the way the case was dragging on.

Where was I? Ah, Friday night telly. You could tell what day it was from the telly, not like now where it's the same shows every night. It was so far back that *Coronation Street* wasn't on some days. As it happened, I didn't manage to see all that much of it. I was just about to head to the chippy when I saw a little red Mini pull up next to my window and there was a knock on the van door.

DC Holt.

As ever she was in plain clothes, but the general effect was a bloody sight less plain than usual. She'd let her hair down, and it was hanging over her shoulders. Nice shade of blonde it was, probably had a catchy name on the bottle, but blonde will do. She was wearing a nice bright yellow and blue dress which might have been considered a little too much for the Tenby CID, but seemed rather fetching to me. Showed off her figure a damn sight better than the brown twin-set she'd had on earlier. Nice figure it was too. Probably go pear-shaped after the first kid, but that was all in the future.

No, I really mean 'pear-shaped'. Welsh mothers have big bottoms. Aye, you can print that, my mother certainly won't be reading it where she is. Fahrenheit 451 and all that. Hehehe.

You don't read much, do you? Ray Blackberry, Mz T.

Back to my surprise guest.

I asked what I could do for her.

"Well, it's more what we can do for each other, I was thinking."

Hmmm.

"I thought maybe if we both spent some time talking the case over, we might come up with some new ideas."

Now, of course, there should have been a 'sir' in there somewhere, but I hadn't heard one. I pointed out that I was hungry and just about to head off to the chippy.

"Good idea, cod and chips for me, salt and plenty of vinegar. While you're gone, I'll pop these in the fridge."

She had four bottles of Mackeson in a plastic bag.

Well, off to the chippy then, with plenty to think about. It seemed Cardiff girls were a little faster than I was used to. Mind you, nothing like the photos you see of Queen Street at the weekend now, skirts up their arses, knickers round their ankles and collapsed in the street in a pool of their own puke. No wonder half of them end up in hospital. Half of them pregnant by the time they're in the fifth form. Dunno what their parents are doing letting their kids out to behave like that. Not that I've been anywhere near Cardiff for donkey's years now, but Eastbourne is probably the same. No, fair enough, I'm not one to risk a town centre on a Saturday night anymore. Any night really, the older I get the more I appreciate the home comforts.

As it turned out DC Holt had her chips under false pretences, since it turned out that she had no new ideas about the case at all. Suppose I could have demanded my 1/6d back, but costing in the stouts we probably came out of it about even. Mind you, she then got outside a good few glasses of my best whisky which put her back in my debt again, as I pointed out. She said she couldn't be bought for a few drinks.

On the other hand, it appeared she could be borrowed.

All told quite an interesting evening, though there was probably something in the Policeman's Rule Book against it. Fortunately neither of us had a copy of it on us.

'Taking advantage of my position'? Dunno what you mean, it was her position that seemed the advantageous one, from what I remember.

Suicide blonde she was…dyed by her own hand…hehehe!

Next day was Saturday, and since my enquiry into the suicides wasn't held to be urgent it didn't warrant paying overtime, so I managed a lie-in. So did DC Holt, though hers ended before mine as she drove off to Cardiff to see her mam and dad. Normally she went up on Friday night, but she told them she'd had to assist the Inspector with his investigations. That was one way of putting it, I suppose.

Of course, I could have driven back to Barry, but the truth was I couldn't be arsed. Since I wasn't there to supervise the duty rotas, Jane's time off didn't coincide with mine. I was buggered if I was driving two hundred miles there and back just for some of Mother's cooking, when I could just pop down a local café and ask them to let the meal go cold for an hour then shove lumpy gravy on it.

So a weekend on the Pembrokeshire coast it was to be, especially since the weather was looking lovely. Spot of lunch, then I walked it off along the Coastal Path. I think it's a National Park or something now, and I'm bloody sure I couldn't walk ten miles in an afternoon now. Ended up at Amroth for a cream tea. Then all the way back again. Tried to keep fit, as I've mentioned before, just in case I had to chase some crook one day, not that it happened often. I was still playing rugby then, so not in bad shape.

That evening I wandered round a few pubs, can't remember the names of them, probably all changed now anyway. I never understand why breweries always want to change stuff. Some pub has been *The Red Lion'*or the *General Picton* for a hundred years, why bother changing it to *Brahms and Lizt* or *'Staggerz'* or whatever. Take out all the seats and tables and try to fill it with flashing lights and drunken kids. All a bit quieter back then, of course, a pub was a pub not just a warehouse with a bar.

Quite a few pints I had, I used to put the beer away pretty well in my youth, though nowadays I'm more of a spirits man.

Well yes, thanks, if you're going. Bit less tonic this time.

Where were we? Ah yes, Saturday night round the pubs of Tenby. Talked to a few people, barmen and customers about the case. Not that they knew there was a case, a couple of suicides a month or so back hadn't made much of an impression. They all remembered the Mayor's death mind you. He was quite a regular in one or two of the local watering holes, though he wasn't much of a water drinker. 'Bit of a boy'... 'Liked a whisky or two...or four' ...'Definitely a ladies' man.'... 'Anything in a skirt'... 'Dirty old goat'... depending on who was talking of course, but you get the picture.

Nobody at all mentioned depression or suicidal tendencies. Far from it, the news had come as a complete shock. I didn't know whether they realized they were talking to a policeman, I didn't flash the Warrant Card, but a lot of people in my life have told me I look just like a copper. Maybe it's the feet. I wasn't really asking questions, just nudging the conversation the way I wanted and letting people talk. By the end of it I had much the same opinion of the late mayor as I'd been given by his wife. Liked a few drinks and not to be trusted, especially round women.

What? I resent that, I was no tom. Perhaps a little easily led, especially where Welsh policewomen were concerned, but I didn't go looking for it. I might have had an offer or two that very night from the odd Birmingham girl, but I took myself back to the caravan alone just after closing time.

Yes, pubs used to close in the sixties my dear. Last orders at ten thirty, then ten minutes to drink up and out you go. Might have been eleven in Tenby in the summer, don't remember. I don't suppose anyone cares now.

Poor Margaret still lives with her parents. Probably never got over me. A nice girl, but no looks. She had a few friends at school, other musicians and the religious ones. Never had any time for religion myself, but the Christians never did me any harm. It wasn't them I'd be going back for.

I got up earlyish on the Sunday and toddled off to Church. I don't normally bother God, but I didn't mind a bit of singing. Nice enough baritone I had in those days. Yes, it was that Church. The Reverend Probert hadn't been replaced yet, so there was a locum doing the preaching...if priests have locums...or locae. I think I just wanted to see where he'd operated, but I didn't learn anything. Usual congregation, even in those days it was mostly older people. Sunday best, of course. Suits and ties for the men and the women had swapped the lumpy headscarves for hats.

I saw a few people I knew by sight, though it's not that easy to recognise women in hats, cuts off the top of the face. Probert's housekeeper was there, and the woman who'd found Hopkins's body. Seemed a bit much to believe they were in it together. Maybe a few of the neighbours we'd interviewed as we went along too. One middle-aged woman looks pretty much like another when it's the young ones you're interested in...and yes, I know that was ageist, and probably sexist too, use your red pen, Mz T.

The ladies of the Church had laid on a cup of tea in the Church Hall afterwards, so I popped over. It was the only drink I was likely to get in Wales on a Sunday. I had a little word with Mrs Whatever who used to keep house for Probert, and we agreed that it was a terrible thing, and him so young. One or two of the other ladies recognized me better than I did them and we had much the same conversation. Then someone a little younger introduced herself.

*Inspector Williams, isn't it? Mrs Whatever pointed you out to me and said you were the policeman looking into poor Reverend Probert. My name's Margaret Evans, I'm the organist here."

A real Church Mouse was our Margaret. Plain as a bread scone. Hair in a bun, round glasses, tweed skirts and a figure like two aspirins on an ironing board…yes, yes, alright. Atheistically challenged, if you prefer. As somebody said, women turn to God when the Devil has no bloody use for them.

"It was terrible, him dying like that. Nobody round here could understand. Awful, it was."

I asked her if she'd known him well.

"Well, yes and no."

Come on, love, make a decision, which was it.

"Well, I'd actually been at school with him. Funny really, anyone less likely to be a vicar you couldn't have met, in fact I didn't like him very much at all back then. Bit of a nasty boy. Then I didn't see him for donkey's years, though I did hear he became a vicar, but I hardly believed it. Then he came here."

And he'd made his old school friend organist? Poor sod fancied getting into her pants?

"Oh no, nothing like that."

She meant the first question, she'd probably have fainted if I'd actually asked the second one.

"No, I'd already been organist here for a couple of years. Took over from old Mr Thomas quite unexpected, he actually dropped dead in the middle of 'Who Would True Valour See' at evening service, just at the bit about the Hobgoblins. Old Reverend Morrison was a bit put out as he never got to deliver his sermon."

I was beginning to see that Miss Evans wasn't much of a conversationalist as well as not much of a looker. Yes, Miss Evans, definitely Miss. Back to the conversation, I assumed she was as puzzled as anyone else by Probert's demise.

"None of us can believe it. You see, when he came to the parish he was like a completely different person from the one I'd remembered. So kind, thoughtful. You could really see the Holy Spirit in him. A true man of God. I'll never believe he did it himself, he'd have thought it a terrible sin."

I assumed she had no alternative theory, but it appeared she'd given it thought.

"Well, I was wondering if maybe he'd been cleaning the oven, or trying to light it and fainted or something."

I think somebody'd proposed something similar at the inquest, which had maybe been an attempt to put enough doubt in the jury's mind for that open verdict. I suppose nobody wanted a Reverend buried in unconsecrated ground.

Fortunately I'd finished my tea by then, so I didn't need to listen to any more of her wittering. I might even have burned my mouth throwing it down so fast and I wandered away to get another cup and a biscuit. Lincolns they were, but I suppose the Church wasn't too flush. Tea was bloody weak as well. The word had got round that there was a policeman in their midst and I was button-hooked by a few more members of the congregation, all of whom had much the same things to say. Dreadful loss, couldn't understand it, seemed so happy in the parish, perfectly normal at Evensong.

So much for my devotions, probably the last time I set foot inside a Welsh Church until Mother's funeral.

Time for me to go, I fear, somewhere I need to be. See you next time my dear.

Sorry.

No, my shout this time, young man. Ms T off with Justine Bleeder again?

Oh, well, I'm sorry she feels that way. 'Dinosaur' seems a bit harsh, though I'll admit I'm not much of a fan of all that PC stuff. It's like pretending that if you talk nicely about shit it'll stop smelling. Call a spade a spade I say. Still, I won't be around to offend young lady reporters for much longer, I dare say.

Shall we get on with it?

Monday, and DC Holt showed up for another of our waste of time trips. Remember Bowen, who poisoned himself with nicotine? Well, we were off to see his sister in Penarth. DC Holt was a bit cheesed off to be driving up there after just returning from her parents' the night before, but she coped. Not so flirtatious that day, sensible girl, kept her mind on the road.

Nice big house Mrs Bryan lived in. I may have mentioned she'd married a solicitor, or as she was pleased to tell us, the senior partner in Wilson, Bryan, Smedley and Rees, one of Cardiff's best known firms. I'd never heard of them, but was informed snootily that they never touched criminal work.

I didn't warm to her. Nose in the air, proper Penarth snob she was. 'All fur coat and no knickers,' as my Nan used to say. Still, that didn't mean she'd driven down to Saundersfoot and poisoned her brother's gin.

"I didn't see a great deal of my brother, Mr Williams. We moved in rather different circles, and I didn't care to visit Saundersfoot. My sister-in-law and I were not the best of friends. One hesitates to speak ill of the dead, but she didn't really come from a very good family. I believe her father was a publican. I think they spent most of their time socialising at the local rugby club. My brother was always very enthusiastic about rugby. Nasty violent game."

Oh, so her brother had been a violent man?

"Oh no, nothing like that. I believe his aggression was confined to the game, though he did get into trouble now and again at school, but then boys will be boys."

So he'd stopped beating his wife?

"Oh, I'm sure there was never anything like that. They were quite the devoted little couple."

She made it sound like an insult. But then I was fairly sure she could have made most things sound contemptuous. Nasty woman. Though even she couldn't find a reason why her brother would have killed himself.

"None at all. He always seemed to be enjoying life hugely, quite the life and soul of the party. Life and soul of any occasion."

Well, I'd met a few 'life and souls' in my time, and I'd sooner be nowhere near the buggers. Generally means a nasty loudmouthed piece of work, always looking for someone to make a mean joke at. rugby clubs were full of them.

Well, yes, I did, but it was the game I liked, not the bloody hangers-on. Committee-men, always full of their own importance. Never been in a club since I got too old to play. Well, never mind rugby, let's stick with Mrs Bryan, though we were pretty much finished. I mentioned the will.

"Yes, we did inherit quite a substantial sum, and the Saundersfoot house will be sold soon. Not that we have any problems in that area, my husband comes from a very well-known family and the firm has been highly successful for over a hundred years."

She was right about that, we checked later on. Well, rule one of investigating anything is never to believe what anyone tells you.

To make sure we had the full set, we stopped off on the way back to see Ken Hughes in Carmarthen. Hughes's Motors he was, had the big Rootes dealership for West Wales and a string of flash showrooms in all the major towns. I suppose you won't remember the Rootes Group. They made all the Hillmans and Humbers, Singers and Sunbeams. Nice reliable cars for nice reliable people. I had a Hillman Minx myself once. I doubt you'd get away with using that name for a car now. They went to the wall in the seventies, when the government forced them to build their new factory in Scotland and everything had to make a six hundred mile round trip to be assembled. But probably Ken

Hughes had made his pile by then.

He was very much the self-made man, as he was happy to keep telling us, built his business up from a garage in New Hedges. He was much fonder of the Bowens than Mrs Bryan had been.

"Lovely people, never heard a word said against them. Helped me out with a loan towards my first little showroom, paid back long since, with interest, though they never asked for any."

That seemed a little odd for a bank manager, they're not known for offering interest-free loans.

"No, he said he couldn't do it through the bank, not enough security, so it was just a personal thing. Got it all back inside six months. I offered him a partnership, but he said he was happy with the bank. That and the rugby club...he loved the game. Hated to have to give up, but his knees had gone."

I had a sniff of an idea there and asked if Bowen had been in a lot of pain lately, but Hughes quashed that.

"No, he could walk around fine, but eighty minutes of running, tackling, twisting and turning and he could hardly get out of bed the next day. Nobody beats old age."

The beat word set me off on another track.

"Oh no, never any trouble between them. I liked him fine, but I'd have shot the bugger if I'd heard of anything like that. But they seemed a devoted couple. Met at school and together ever since. I still can't believe it. It must have been some sort of ghastly accident, they had everything to live for, and not an enemy in the world."

I wondered if he'd been a more frequent visitor than Mrs Bryan.

"Oh yes, we used to see each other twice a month for Sunday lunch. We'd go down there or they'd come up to us…my wife, Glenys and me. Not much apart from that in recent years, we weren't the rugby type, nor golf either. I think he'd been playing quite a lot of golf since his knees."

The will?

"Yes, there wasn't one of course, and with them dying together it might have been a little awkward, but his sister's husband sorted it all out, I think the taxman took a pretty big bite, and then we shared it out. Less his executor's fees of course."

Hmmm….might have thought he'd have waived those for his own brother-in-law's estates, especially since he was trousering a good sum from it.

"Hah! Touching faith you have in human nature, Inspector. Ever know a solicitor to fart without charging you for it?"

No, nor a used car salesman who could be trusted, but I decided not to mention that. Still, Hughes had also gathered in a fair few quid.

"Well, I did, but I was hardly on my uppers, and money wasn't important next to Val. We'd always looked after each other and we were all that was left after mum and dad died. Now she's gone too…and the bugger of it is that I can't make any bloody sense of it at all. It was completely out of the blue…we'd always talked over any little problem, but never a word about anything…and then this."

It's always meant to be a shame to see a grown man cry. I've seen it far more often than you'd believe. Poor sod. I think it was the not understanding that ate away at him.

Well, that was all the families and beneficiaries talked to. Of course, we'd checked on their whereabouts and none of them was anywhere near the scene of their relatives' suicides. And yes, we'd seen *Strangers On A Train,* so we even gave a little thought to the possibility of swapping victims, but we couldn't make that work. You could hardly credit the idea of the Proberts pouring nicotine into the Bevans while Mrs Hopkins was gassing His Reverence.

The road from Carmarthen to Tenby was quite a quiet one, so it seemed that DC Holt didn't need to concentrate that hard.

"So, Inspector Williams. You courting?"

"I know a young lady in Barry. What about you, Detective Constable."

"I know a young man in Cardiff, though he's in Germany at the moment. Royal Welch Fusiliers."

"Perhaps it's useful to keep in practice."

"Maybe. While the cat's away, eh?"

I wasn't sure that Jane would take to being referred to as 'the cat', but then I didn't plan to pass it on.

It was Monday though, so she dropped me at the van and took herself off to her lodgings, and I settled down to watch Hughie Green make Opportunity Knock for somebody or other.

That little bastard. He was the worst of the lot. The others maybe were just kids and stupid, but he was old enough to know better. He could have stopped it, but he made it so much worse instead. I swore I'd make him suffer, and I knew how too.

By now I'd left the Commandos, and I thought maybe I might go back to Pharmacy, but I decided I knew enough. It was time to get started. Tracking them down wasn't difficult, just took patience, questions here and there. Do you know, nobody recognised me? Been away so long and changed so much. No more little fat Spaz with the big specs. Contact lenses I had now, six foot two I was. No trouble for me to deal with anybody I needed to.

Little bastard.

It was a couple of days later then we heard about number five.

This one was up at Killgetty, a village the other side of Saundersfoot. Another unexplained death, though from the sound of it nothing suspicious. I don't remember where DS Watson was, but they let me have DS Price. Malcolm Price, or as they all called him, Half-Price.

Well, I've mentioned police humour, so you'll guess he wasn't the tallest of men. Some people suggested he'd borrowed his wife's high heels when he took the entry test. Yes, there used to be a minimum height requirement. Five foot eight I think it was, and Half-Price had probably scraped in by a hair. Course, these days that's all out the window and they'd take the bloody Seven Dwarves if they were the right colour. Or the Seven Vertically Disadvantaged Goldminers, whatever you have to call them now.

Now I'm not a racist, young man and I'm all for letting the Ethnic Minors and the differently-abled get a fair crack of the whip, but you have to keep standards up. You look at the Indian and Pakistan cricket teams, there's no shortage of well set up blokes in there, so there was no need to start taking in all the smaller blokes. I've seen coppers the size of kids walking about. All well and good if Granny's throwing bread for the ducks and you want to arrest her for littering, but it's no good for breaking up a fight in Tiger Bay on a Saturday. And then they abolished the fitness tests, because it discriminated against the unfit or something. You see some coppers who look like they spend all their duty time in the canteen. No wonder they had to get rid of the proper uniforms, kit them all out in road-menders' jackets and baseball caps.

Ignore me son, erase it. I'm an old man, but it breaks my heart to see what they've done to the police force. Now it's a service, championing diversity and delivering a quality product to all sections of the community without discrimination and in a spirit of true equality. If you ask me, most sections of the community would be a bloody sight happier if the police went back to catching criminals.

Still, nobody ever does ask me. Or ever will again.

What set me off? Oh yes, Half-Price. He wasn't the brightest penny in the pile either. Half-Wit Price might have been just as accurate, but a little too cruel even for a police nick-name. In case I needed someone with a brain, we took DC Holt as well. She was back in something more businesslike and with her hair up again. She seemed to have the sense not to refer to the fish supper episode.

Up to Killgetty. What they call a cottage now, though in those days we'd have called it a terraced house. Your standard two up two down, though it had a bathroom built onto the back, which was progress and luxury indeed. My grandmother never had an indoor toilet in her life, and baths were generally hanging on the back wall and brought in on a Sunday night to be filled in front of the kitchen fire.

A tidy enough little place it was, full of old sports

trophies and rugby photos, from which I detected that the late lamented had been something of a sportsman in his youth. His youth was quite a way behind him. Seventy odd he was, or had been, which fouled up any vague idea of the suicides being linked by age.

Yes, young man, I am getting things a little out of order here. I'm generally more organised if I'm not feeling dry, so perhaps another one of these?

Nice. Cheers.

Handel Jenkins was the deceased's name, and he was hanged by the neck until he be dead. In fact when we got there, he was still hanging, since nobody'd told the constables to cut him down and the quack hadn't turned up yet.

Yes, normally they would have cut him down and tried to revive him, but one look told you he was way past that. His neck wasn't on straight and he was as cold as a Caerphilly Christmas. Probably been there a couple of days. There had been three days' milk on the doorstep, which had worried his neighbour. She'd been even more worried when he didn't answer the door. And pretty bloody frantic when she'd looked through the letter box and seen his feet dangling in the hall. Mrs Edwards her name was, but we'll come back to her later.

To my detective's eye, it appeared that he'd tied one end of a decent sized rope round the banister, the other end in a serviceable noose round his neck, then climbed over the banister and jumped.

Naturally I couldn't expect the Doc to examine him *in shitoo* so I arranged the cutting down. I let Blondie do the cutting bit while Half-Price and I did the catching.

No....of course, quite right...DC Holt. Yes, I wouldn't want your readers to think I was disrespectful of my female colleagues. Dinosaur, young man, that's me. You put it right, eh?

We got him down and laid out in the hall. Quite a little old bloke he was. Dressed tidily enough, suit, collar and tie, but then that wasn't unusual back then. Not all football shirts and baseball caps like these days. I detected that he supported the RNLI since he had one of their flags in his lapel. Again, not unusual, of course, most people round coastal towns support them. There seemed nothing of much interest in his pockets, and by now the quack had arrived to use his years of experience to advise us that we had a dead man on our hands. Dead about two days he thought, which fitted in with the milk. Death probably due to a broken neck, though he might have said something about cervical vertebrae or some such. Probable cause was hanging, though we'd need the post mortem to be sure.

As usual we took a very good look around the place, for all the bloody good it did us. The late Mr Jenkins was keen on sport as I said, all the photos of him from rugby days, as a player and a club member, depending on whether he was wearing a jersey or a blazer.

What? Yes, I did say he was a little bloke, but you

don't have to be the size of Arnold Shagganegger to play rugby. Probably been a scrum-half from the look of him, though not for many years. Looked well over seventy to me.

No note of course, but we were getting pretty used to that by now. Nothing at all out of the ordinary in his little house. It was kept pretty neat and tidy, all the washing up was done, all his clothes were hanging neatly in the wardrobe, nothing out of place apart from the milk. He had a very small garden out the back, a few rose bushes and a postage stamp of a lawn. A little shed too, but nothing much in it apart from a bottle of spray for the roses. Might have contained nicotine, I can't remember, but he hadn't chosen to use it so it probably didn't matter.

Time for a chat to his neighbour, yes, the one who'd called us. Mrs Edwards? Mrs Edmonds? Can't remember now, she wasn't important, just some old lady, probably in curlers. As I said before, she'd seen the milk out and taken a peek, then couldn't call us fast enough. She'd been living next door about twenty years, but only really knew him to nod at and say good morning. She'd been friendly with his wife, who'd died about five years before. Evelyn Jenkins. But old Handel had never been the type to socialise with the neighbours. Not women neighbours at any rate…or at least not old ones like her, for all I knew he was the Casanova of Kilgetty. But we could find that out later.

Same old questions.

"No sir, I hadn't noticed him being particularly upset,

but then I didn't see him all that often. Just in passing. I know he was very upset when his wife died. Lovely woman Evelyn, everybody liked her. She'd been a teacher too, that's where he met her I suppose."

"Ah, Mr Jenkins was a teacher?"

"Well, used to be. Retired now these years. PE I think he was. Loved his sport, he did. Used to go up the rugby club every Saturday for a pint or two."

"Taught at the grammar school, did he?"

That was from Half-Price who was local, I had no idea about schools in Tenby.

"Oh no, love. Up at The College."

Well, that needed an explanation, so I got one. St David's College, Tenby it was. On the road out towards Narbeth, one of the leading public schools in Wales. The Welsh Eton, according to the locals, and I dare say the school itself did nothing to discourage the comparison. Boarding and day pupils, mostly boys but girls in the sixth form. It's still there, but probably has girls all the way through now. Actually I know it does, I got my grandson to Joogle it last night.

Routine and more routine, we asked all the neighbours and got the same story. Nobody had known him all that well, they'd been more friendly with his wife, who'd been an absolute saint by all accounts. I got the impression that maybe she'd needed to be, but nobody was saying anything definite to his detriment. A trip up the Rugby Club seemed indicated, but that wouldn't be open on a Thursday morning. We asked about relatives, but none of the neighbours knew of any.

For what it was worth we later found out that he'd been the youngest of his family and his brothers were dead. He wasn't rich, but the house was worth a bit. His heir was a nephew in Australia. Yes, he really was in Australia, and hadn't popped over on a boat to lynch his uncle. Dot the 't's and cross the 'i's as ever.

Of course, we didn't know that at the time, so I had the bright idea of driving up to the College to see if anyone remembered him and could point us at some friends and relatives.

I left Half-Price in charge of the scene of the crime, in the unlikely event there had been one, and DC Blondie...whoops, sorry...Holt drove me up there...never liked driving myself if I could avoid it. Might have mentioned that before. I tend to repeat myself more these days, Jane was always picking me up on it.

I dare say you haven't seen the place, but it was impressive. Dated back to the eighteenth century I found out, huge great building, set in acres of grounds. Plenty of sports fields, and the smell of money. Bit different from Barry Grammar where I'd got my eduction.

We saw the Headmaster. Mason, I think his name was. He looked about a hundred years old, so I was hoping he'd remember Jenkins, and he did.

"Ah, yes, Mr Jenkins. I remember him well. Retired about eight years ago, I think. He'd been here about forty years. Much longer than I. Very dedicated. Took his sport very seriously. Did wonders for the First Fifteen. I believe he'd played for Llanelli in his younger days. Always took his sport very seriously. One of the old school, stood no nonsense. Very serious about his sport."

Well, you could make of that what you wanted, but it didn't seem too helpful, despite the repetition. Not that I was expecting much, seemed unlikely that he'd topped himself over anything that happened at school. Mind you, these days it seems that forty year old allegations are all the rage, but that's only famous people they can try to screw compensation out of. No teachers, plumbers or vicars need worry.

Well, alright, perhaps some of the stars might have been a bit lax checking birth certificates back in the sixties, but it's a bloody long time ago. Yes, we'll stick to the point I suppose. None of my business now anyway, I've been retired a damned sight longer than eight years. Still. Let's hope DC Holt doesn't show up and claim I forced myself on her in a caravan fifty years ago. Not worth suing me on a police pension in any case. And then she is dead, which makes it even less likely.

I hadn't expected to learn much at the college, and I

didn't. Lots of people remembered Jenkins, but the ones that did hadn't been close friends and the ones who'd been friends weren't there anymore. He'd been pretty thick with two other blokes in the PE department, but they'd moved on to pastures new, one in Manchester and the other in North Wales. Didn't seem worth contacting them. The place was just about to break up for the summer, and I think most of the teachers had pretty much had a gutsful by then. The ones who'd known him said how sorry they wers, though I didn't get the feeling they'd be shedding too many tears. The general impression I had was that he was mad keen on sport and, of course, nobody had any idea why he might top himself.

I got DC Holt to call Half-Price to see if he could find any medicine bottles in Jenkins's place. He could, with labels from the Kilgetty surgery, so we dropped in there on the way back for a word with his GP. Luckily he was in, rather than out on his calls. Huh, that was a long time ago, when you'd call the quack and he'd trot round to see you that morning. Last time my wife was taken ill the surgery offered me an appointment the following month if I drove her in. Called the ambulance instead. There's some advice for you, son, if anyone in your family gets took queer, never bother with the doctor, just call an ambulance. They have to come and they'll probably take you straight to hospital. Good blokes too and they all speak bloody English.

Fair play, son, you've got plenty of patience with an old fart's ramblings.I know I go on a bit. No bugger ever listens any more, mind you.

Anyway, Jenkins's doctor was as helpful as he could be after I'd mentioned he'd just been found dead.

"Didn't see him very much, Inspector. He fell and broke a finger last year, and walked up here to have it bandaged. Didn't want to be a trouble to the hospital. Trouble with rheumatism and arthritis, particularly his knees, so he had tablets for that. Pretty normal for old people, especially old sportsmen. Not much we can do about it, except tablets for the pain. My receptionist lives near him, told me he'd got a bit quieter since his wife died, but he never talked about that to me. Stiff upper lip I suppose. He mentioned he was having trouble getting off to sleep, so I gave him some sleeping tablets too. God, he didn't take an overdose, did he?"

All I could say was that it didn't appear so, we had to be careful with opinions. Any reason to think that Mr Jenkins might have done away with himself?

"Well, if they'd just found him dead at home, old bloke in his seventies, I'd probably have been called and you wouldn't be here asking questions."

Fair point, finding an old boy dead at home is no great surprise, not usually. The Doc didn't have any more ideas.

"No, I didn't know him well at all, his wife died five years ago...cancer, been ill a while. I saw him then, of course, but he wasn't the type to pour his heart out. Didn't strike me as the suicidal type…but who knows, eh? Maybe he just got tired and lonely and had enough."

Which is exactly what we'd have thought, if he hadn't been the fifth suicide in two months. Suicide was exactly what it looked like, according to the pathologist. There was no trace of any drugs or drink in him, no other sign of violence. It seemed he'd put his suit on, climbed the stairs, tied himself a noose, tied the other end to the banister and jumped over.

I was surprised the banister hadn't broken. "Not that much of him really," said the pathologist, "and the banister was solid wood, nice strong job. As I say, he was a little bloke, and it looked like he hadn't been feeding himself all that well. Only just eight stone. Prostate cancer too, but he might well not have known about it. Most old men die with it, but not of it. Whatever, the broken neck killed him, second and third cervical vertebra broken. Bit unusual, it's usually the fourth and fifth that go with a proper judicial hanging. Still, it's not an exact science, and I assume he hadn't had chance to practise much."

God save us all from Doctor's bloody jokes. They make policemen look funny. I'm getting a bit out of order here, the post-mortem came later. We had a bit more digging about to do first. I was entitled to a DS while I was investigating a suspicious death, so Half-Price and I went down the rugby club that night. DC Holt didn't come, I'm not sure whether the rugby club admitted women except on 'Ladies'

Nights'. Of course, they couldn't have kept a policewoman out, but I decided it was no place for a lady. Yes, I do realise that's sexist, but bear in mind they hadn't invented sexism then so it wasn't a problem.

We saw the steward first, who made all the appropriate noises, terrible shame, such a shock, not many of the old school left and so on. I asked about Jenkins's habits.

"Regular as clockwork he was, sir. Every night, bar Sunday of course, he was in at nine. He'd have two halves of bitter and be gone by half past ten. Dunno where he used to put them though, he was only a little *dwt* of a bloke. Nothing of him. Been a hell of a scrum half when he was young, but got even smaller these last few years. Not too good at cooking for himself, maybe. I heard his wife died a few years ago."

I asked about special friends.

"Not so many now, I'm afraid. A lot of that generation gone, some nights he was sat in the corner all by himself with the paper, though the barmaids would try to jolly him along. Not all that easy to jolly really. If old Dr Roberts was in they'd usually sit and have a chat."

And where might two thirsty policemen find old Dr Roberts?

"Well, if he's coming in, he'll be here about half past nine. I would offer you a pint while you're waiting, but I suppose you're on duty."

I decided to take myself off duty for long enough to sink a pint and offered Price one. He said a half would do him nicely, maybe that's where he got the nickname? I thought I'd see if the DS had any views on the case.

"Looks bloody obvious to me, like, sir. Got fed up without his wife, put on a suit and tie to look good for the undertaker an 'ung 'isself."

Well, not the most eloquent summing-up, but I couldn't find a flaw in it. The steward nodded at us and pointed to a chubby, white-haired old boy in a blazer who'd walked in while I was listening to Half-Price. I assumed this must be Doctor Roberts.

"Yes, that's right, Hywel Roberts and you'll be the police, judging from those feet. About poor bloody Handel, I suppose."

So he'd heard.

"You must be joking, mun. All over the village about two minutes after you arrived. Suicide, they say."

Certainly that was one theory, though our enquiries were not yet complete and all that. I understood he was friendly with the deceased.

"Yes, we'd known each other a long time. Played in the same teams when he was a little heavier and I was a bloody sight lighter. Always had a drink together if we were in. Not that Handel had much to say, he'd gone very quiet since his wife died. Sad business that was. Cancer, and took a while. He'd been pretty keen to talk rugby in the old days, even cricket in the summer. Loved his sport, did Handel."

I was beginning to get the impression he'd liked sport. So he'd been depressed since his wife's death?
"Well now, I'm not sure I'd say depressed, but definitely quieter. Not sure he knew what to do with himself. He wasn't really ever a sociable man, and the few old mates he had are all dead now except me. He was a bit lost, really."

Not the most friendly of men then?

"He was alright, hard little bugger he'd been on the rugby field, and a bit of a tartar as a PE teacher, I'm told by some of the lads here who'd been taught by him. Bit of a temper, he could have. Bit of shouting round their house now and then, so old Mrs Edwards told my wife. No real harm in him though. I shall be sorry not to see the old sod again."

Not a happy marriage then?

"Oh, no, I'm not saying that, mun. They seemed alright. She'd been a teacher up at the College too for a bit, though she gave it up after they married. Getting on they were when that happened…he was well over fifty. Seemed alright when he brought her to Ladies' nights down here, and he was very broken up to see her go."

Well, the question was, how broken up?

"I wouldn't have said he was the suicidal type at all. Probably have seen it as the coward's way out. I was very surprised to hear it, we'd been talking last week, and it was all 'See you next time, Doc' when he left. Very strange."

Had Roberts ever prescribed anything for him?

"Oh no, I was never his doctor, up with James at the Health Centre he was, not that he ever went. Didn't have much time for the medical profession. 'Useless buggers. Poke you about, cut you to bits, fill you full of tablets and you die all the bloody same. No shape to them at all.' I didn't bother disagreeing, I've been retired ten years now."

I was getting tired of hearing the same thing about all the cases. No reason to kill themselves, never talked about it or showed any tendencies, no note, yet here we were with five of them inside two months.

I was beginning to think that maybe the statistics were just wrong, and this was a bumper year for people to top themselves. Nothing else made sense, there were no signs of murder, no strange pacts, no connection between the corpses, and really nothing to go on.

I was bloody nowhere with it, I wanted to go home, pack my bags and get started on my transfer to the Met. There was no case at all, just some daft coincidence to get me chasing my tail and wasting my time. Sometimes people just have enough and top themselves. Even in quiet little places like

Pembrokeshire.

Good Lord, is that the time? I'll have to be going son, see you soon. Can't miss visiting hours. No, son. Not the hospital. Wish it was.

Nice to see you young man, come in, sit down, yes, the sofa will do. Can I get you a drink?

Here you are, and a drop for myself. Don't tell the quack, he says gin and painkillers don't mix. In fact he says that gin doesn't mix too well with being my age, if I want to get any older. I think given the choice, I'll stick with the gin.

Hang on, let's get the leg up. No, not broken, thank God, just badly sprained but I'm not exactly sprinting about. Patch of ice coming out of the Eastbourne Con Club last week. Perhaps I should call one of them no win/no shame lawyers off the telly and sue the buggers for gross negligées.

Good of you to come round, though I'm not sure why you bother really. Wouldn't it be faster to Joogle some of my old cases, rather than hear me drag it out ?

Well, yes there is the eye-witness thing, but we both know most of it'll get edited out before you print it. If any of it ever gets into print.

Hrmph. I suppose it might make some kind of a novel, not that I'll be writing it. English never was my stronghold. Still, even Joogle won't give you the full facts on this one. I'm probably the only one left alive who knows the truth behind it all. Maybe you best hope I stay alive long enough to tell you, or you'll never write your novel.

Well, another little top-up and I'll get on with it.

No, it's just the two of us, Mrs Williams isn't here today.

We ended up exactly where we'd been all along, nowhere. My copperly nose was twitching at all these suicides in the same area in such a short time, so was Jeff Jones's. I dunno which bits of Veronica Holt were twitching, but she'd paid another couple of evening visits to my caravan for some fish supper. Prime cod in Saundersfoot, and she generally brought something to wash it down with. Inventive girl, I reckon she must have read that Kamikaze Sutra.

What?

No, I think my title sounds better... I was surely on a suicide mission if Jane found out.

At least we'd decided to keep it discreet in Saundersfoot, so there were no Saturdays on the beach for the two of us, nor evenings out in the local pub. Nobody ever noticed that little red Mini parked outside my caravan every now and again.

I did have one little brain wave, which was to wonder whether I'd actually started at the beginning. I mean, the Bowen suicides were the first ones to come to our attention, but perhaps there'd been others before them, so I got DC Holt to look into all the files for suicides that year. We found three.

A farmer out near Haverfordwest had got into money problems and his wife had left him. Blew his head off with a shotgun. Left a note, calling his wife a lot of names. Sixty years old he was, found by his son who was also a farmer.

Girl in Milford got herself in the family way by some married bloke and took an overdose. Also left a note, also using a lot of nasty names, which the coroner was pleased to read out at the inquest naming the bloke in question. It seemed his marriage didn't last much longer after that.

Bloke jumped into the sea off the Pembroke cliffs. No note this time, but had just had a very nasty diagnosis from his cancer tests. Divorced, lived alone, a retired builder.

None of them seemed at all unusual, which was why they'd gone unnoticed, and there seemed no point to digging them up again. If you like, they were 'normal' suicides, fitted the pattern. I was surprised not to see a teenager amongst them. Teenagers love topping themselves, makes them feel important, and then they sadly aren't around to enjoy the attention afterwards. Though the girl in Milford had only been twenty.

Huh! Listen to me, 'only twenty'. She'd be popping out her fourth at twenty these days, and demanding a bigger council house for them. Certainly wouldn't be feeling any shame over it.

None of them seemed to have anything in common with the ones I was looking at, not that I could find a pattern there either. Different methods, different ages, different jobs, different classes. Nothing seemed to tie them together, nothing any of us could think of.

Until the day Half-Price walked into the office I was using, pulled up a chair and sat down. Looking like the cat who'd got the cream.

"Inspector Williams, I've done it. I've found the connection."

"What connection might that be, Price."

It was a struggle not to use the nick-name, but I was a Detective Inspector, so needed to behave properly. Believe me, I was thinking it though.

"Between the suicides. It's been staring us in the face the 'ole bloody time, see?"

I didn't see, but I assumed he'd get there in the end.

"I've looked back at all of them, and it stares you in the face."

1...   2...   3...   4.....

"I dunno how we missed it."

5... 6... 7... 8... 9...

"Old ladies."

"What?"

"Old ladies, Inspector. Every time."

"What old ladies, Price and when?"

"Just look at the cases, Inspector and ask yourself who found the bodies?' An old lady, every time."

Well. It did have a certain warped logic behind it, I supposed. The Bowens had been found by Edna Perkins, the char. Aneurin Probert by his housekeeper. The neighbour who'd seen the fumes coming out of Hopkins garage door and called the police was female and wouldn't be seeing fifty again, and Jenkins's next door neighbour was another paid-up member of the curlers and house-coat brigade. So far so good, but where the hell did Price think he was going with it?

"See, it fits, doesn't it? We should 'ave seen it at once."

"But what are you suggesting, Price? That it's the same old lady murdering people and making it look like suicide? Or have we got a League Of Murderous Gentlewomen prowling the streets of Pembrokeshire, dedicated to the slaughter of those younger, prettier and wealthier than themselves?"

"Well, that remains to be seen. It'll need to be investigated, of course."

No it bloody wouldn't. I'd read plenty of stupid crime books in my time, but I'd never seen an author daft enough to make a gang of old biddies into serial killers.

Mind you, just to keep him quiet, I did send Half-Price out to re-interview the four old dears in question, see if he could establish some sort of link in his own strange little world. Got nowhere of course, none of them had ever heard of any of the others. According to her neighbour, Edna Perkins had gone off to Pontypridd to nurse her sister who'd been 'took bad' and bloody Half-Price wanted to drive up there to talk to her, but I drew the line at that. I've no idea how the man ever got to be a CID Sergeant. Either he had friends in high places, or he knew where some bodies were buried.

Anyway, what slight interest I had in his ravings soon disappeared, because I actually found a decent, honest-to-God clue a day or two later.

Hah! I'll just leave you in suspenders there while I pop to the bathroom. Stick a little more gin in my glass, and whatever you're having. Oooof…bugger this ankle. 'I may be gone for some time', as the saying goes.

Back again. Maybe time I looked into having a bathroom put downstairs. Or maybe a bungalow. The ankle's healing up. But the knees and the hips aren't what they used to be. I need to lose some weight, the quack says. Perhaps I'll start running marathons. Not so easy to lose the old *avoirdoopeas* when you can't move around much and eating and drinking are about the only pleasures left to you.

Back to the story...left you on a bit of a cliffdangler there like all the best books. Maybe I should have started writing books when I retired. Lots of policemen do, I'm told, but they probably write like bloody coppers. Too late now.

The pathologists had finished with the mortal remains of Handel Jenkins, and the coroner had signed the burial certificate. Except his will said he was to be cremated and his ashes scattered on the pitch at his local Rugby Club. I assumed he'd asked permission first. That was a little more complicated, since you needed two doctors to sign for a cremation then. I dunno about now, might find out soon enough.

His nephew couldn't be arsed to travel over from Australia for the occasion and it looked as if attendance would be sparse, so since I had nothing to do, I decided to pop along. I took DC Holt, just to keep her out of mischief. She said if it was all the same to me she'd prefer the pictures. Cheeky madam.

So, off to the Narbeth crem it was. Never been to one before. They had a vicar from somewhere to say a few words, though it seemed pretty clear he hadn't known the deceased. Dr Roberts was there, and a couple of other old boys who looked as if they'd played rugby forty years ago and drunk beer down the club ever since. Mason the College headmaster, out of duty I assumed, and two people with him who might have been ex-teachers.

And Ken Hughes.

Ken Hughes, Bowen's brother-in-law. The bloke with the car showrooms.

Well. What was he doing there?

I sat through the hymns, the eulology and then the coffin headed off to the oven and we trooped out. I buttonhooked Hughes and told him I was surprised to see him here.

"Yes, thought I'd turn up and see the old sod off, didn't think there'd be many showed up. He didn't leave the price of a cold meat tea, so why don't we pop across the 'Angel' and I'll buy you and your girlfriend a drink."

Cheeky sod. I think DC Holt said something to him along those lines too.

So, it all came out in the 'Angel'.

"My old rugby master at school. Taught me everything I knew. I was mad keen on the game and played for Llanelli Seconds for a couple of years after school. Couldn't put the time in once the business took off, but I never forgot him. Only a little bloke, but hard as nails he was. Didn't suffer fools, but if you had ability he could bring it out in you."

"So you were at St David's College?"

"Oh yes, both of us, though Val couldn't join till the lower sixth. Three years after me, so we were never there together. Still, pretty soon she had Terry to look after her."

"He was there too?"

"Oh yes, same class as Val, though just for his last two years. Childhood sweethearts and all that."

I asked the obvious question. It seemed far too bloody obvious now.

"No, no idea about a Hopkins or a Probert, plenty of people around with those names though. If they were in Terry's year I wouldn't have noticed them. I would have been an important sixth former, and them just kids."

So, Jenkins would probably have taught Bowen sport too?

"Oh yes, Terry and I often used to chat about the old sod. Now and again we'd bump into him, if Saundersfoot played up at his club. Always had time for a chat. Odd him and Terry and Val going at the same time so unexpectedly."

It was just the one drink we shared. The lovely

Veronica and I had an errand to run.

The College had broken up for the summer, but Mason was still in his office, doing whatever headmasters do after term finishes. He seemed a little surprised to see us again so soon.

"Ah…Inspector…em….er…yes. Delightful to see you again. Good of you to attend the service. Not very many there, I assume most of his family and friends went before him."

I told him what I wanted. He pulled a face which might have meant he was puzzled, or might have meant his breakfast was indigestible. Didn't matter to me either way.

"Yes, yes, of course. I'm sure the ladies in the office will be delighted to help you in any way they can."

So, off to the office, as it were. Neither of the ladies in there seemed at all delighted with our request, but the younger one took us into their records room. It was actually very clean and organized, but it gave the impression that dust and cobwebs might suit it better. I thought maybe the cleaning woman was the only one who'd been in here since the war.
Fair play to the girls, they had a decent filing system, which probably saved us about a day. Everything was in alphabetical order, then cross-referenced by dates. They had Terence Bowen and Valerie Hughes found for us very quickly and Aneurin Probert pretty soon after. Surprise, surprise. Same class. Now, could we go for the jackpot with Michael Hopkins? Oh yes, young man

we could. Another Old Boy and also in the same leaving class.

Bingo.

Yes, of course we should have spotted it earlier, but you don't usually associate suicide with the school that someone's left twenty years before. In fact, even having discovered that rather tenuous link, I couldn't see exactly where it got us. What was there about Tenby College in the forties and fifties that would cause people to start topping themselves in the sixties?

Still, we had something and I wasn't going to let it go until I'd sucked it dry.

Actually, talking of dry…just pass the gin bottle over, would you?

I asked the secretary if they'd all have been taught by Jenkins, but she had no idea. It was certainly possible that the boys would have been, but not Mrs Bowen, Val Hughes as was. Well, obviously the girls didn't use to play rugby. Yes, I know they do now, and are probably very good at it, but not back then. They hadn't invented sexism then, I've told you. Those were the days, though Mrs Williams might not have agreed. Not that she ever wanted to play rugby, as far as I know.

Be that as it was, it was the first connection we'd managed to come across between the suicides, and we weren't going to let it go. First thing I wanted to do was to interview anyone at the school who'd remember that group, but I was out of luck there. Nobody left who would have been teaching at the school then. The forties and early fifties had seen quite a big turnover in staff, for obvious reasons.

What? Well, didn't you study history? There was a war in the forties, lots of teachers had joined up to fight, lots of older blokes had come out of retirement to help out, then there'd been a bit of a shortage after that, so private schools maybe hadn't been able to be too fussy. Things had gone back to normal by the time I was talking about, but it had meant that there were not so many "lifers" around in those decades.

So, it had to be plan B.

First of all I wanted a list of everyone who'd been in that class and their last known address. About fifteen of them there were, since the College kept its sixth form classes small. Four of them had committed suicide that summer. Ten of them I'd never heard of, but there was one name I knew and that was where I was going to start.
The Church Mouse.

A call to Margaret Evans's house established that the dear old spinster still lived with her aged parents, which was no surprise to me. I'll bet my pension she died *vagina untacta* or whatever the phrase is. She worked at Lloyds bank in Pembroke Dock but she'd be home by six.

I wasn't disposed to wait so DC Holt drove me up there. The manager was a little flustered to see the Law showing up unannounced at his branch, but once we'd established that there was no prospect of an imminent robbery and that Miss Evans hadn't done anything wrong, he lent us one of his interview rooms.

"Inspector....I...well...my goodness. This is a surprise. What on earth....I mean...."

There was quite a bit more of that throughout our little chat, but I'll leave most of it out to save time. Miss Evans was definitely flustered, and she seemed a woman who was fairly easy to fluster. I showed her the list and asked if she recognised any of the names on it.

She replied (in essence),

"Yes, of course, they were all the people in my Upper Sixth class when I left St David's College, I told you I was at school with the Reverend Probert."

But she hadn't mentioned the Bowens or Mike Hopkins.
"Well, why would I? People don't normally name their whole class when they say they were at school

with someone."

Well, they might if those people had been found dead in suspicious circumstances too.

"Who? Michael Hopkins and Terry Bowen? What happened to them? I never heard anything?"

It seemed the lady wasn't a great reader of the local papers, or indeed any papers, since her father didn't approve. The news that the Mayor of Tenby had topped himself hadn't reached the wastelands of St Clairs, and nor had the death of the Bowens, which admittedly had been tucked away on page seventeen. In fact she never even knew that Val Hughes had married Bowen.

"We weren't close friends…he was one of the rugby boys, and she was…well, she was a girl who hung around with rugby boys. I was too busy working for my exams and practising my music to have much to do with them. And they pretty much ignored me anyway. Hopkins? Bit of a Flash Harry he was, always one of the girls on his arm. Never bothered with him at all."

And I was pretty sure that Flash Harry Hopkins hadn't bothered noticing the young Miss Evans, poor kid. Maybe nobody ever had.

"I never knew very much about them after I left school. I'm not in touch with anyone from there. Had a big catchment area, so people could live thirty or forty miles apart. Two buses I used to have to take every morning and evening."

"So, you can't tell me what any of those people are doing now?"

"Well. I know Eileen Davis got married just after she left school, her husband was older, in the army. Haydn Lewis, I think was the music teacher at the grammar school, but I don't know if he still is. Couldn't tell you about any of the others. Dreadful thing...to think of four people from my class committing suicide. After all these years. Why?"

Well, that was the sixty-four thousand dollar question, wasn't it? I'd found my link, but I was buggered if it gave me any real answers. Just, as they used to say on Ryan and Ronnie, 'more questions to answer'.

DC Holt seemed quite amused by Miss Evans, for reasons known only to her.

"Can't see your new girlfriend giving Jayne Mansfield too much to worry about. Kind of her to be so keen on God after he's treated her so badly."

I shut her up, I had plenty of thinking to do, and she was getting a bit too lippy for my liking. Trouble with women, they let you in their knickers and they think it gives them all kinds of rights. Yes, yes, yes, red pen time again.

"Keep your mind on the driving please DC Holt, we're going to have a lot of work to get started on when we get back to the nick, And we'll leave poor Miss Evans out of the conversation, thank you."

I wondered how often in her life she'd been referred to as 'poor Miss Evans' or 'poor Margaret'. All that sympathy must have got very wearing. But it seemed DC Holt was not about to let the matter rest. She gave a nasty little smile.

"But I was just wondering, Inspector Williams, Sir, if you thought maybe she done it?"

"Done what?"

"Killed them all. Frustrated spinster, see. Maybe they all turned her down and it's her way of getting revenge."

Well, I supposed it was no stupider than Half-Price's crackpot theory, but not much more plausible either.

"What, even old man Jenkins? And what about Mrs Bowen, did she turn down the prospect of a *manage are Troy* with her husband and the church organist?"

She sniffed, but she wasn't giving up that easily.

"Many a good tune played on an old flute. And maybe she poisoned Mrs Bowen by accident because she drank the same gin as her husband."

Ludicrous.

"That's daft. You must have sex on the brain."

"Well, who put it there, Inspector?"

"Alright, that's enough girl. We're working here, so let's forget about all that for the time being."

Easier said than done in my case, she was an inventive little madam, but I was getting a little worried that the police grapevine might have tendrils that reached Barry Nick, and I had no confidence in Jane's temper if she ever found out. Nor did I want the soldier in Germany to come home and use me for bayonet practice. Perhaps it was time to turn down the fire on DC Holt. If she'd agree to having it turned down.

Of course, she had to have the last word on her theory.

"Anyway, if it wasn't her, perhaps we should be

putting her on suicide watch."

Maybe that wasn't such a stupid suggestion. If something was making her old classmates kill themselves, who knew where the next one might come from?

Back at the Nick it was time for the police to do what they did best.

Legwork.

Since it now seemed that I finally had something to go on, Jeff Jones was happy to slide a little more manpower my way. Nothing much else was happening in Tenby anyway that summer.

I called Half-Price in. I told him to make copies of the list, then get some constables on to tracking down all the people on it. Local stuff they could do in the Panda Cars, but there were a few who'd moved out of the area, so some phoning to other forces might be necessary. The College didn't have the most efficient Old Pupils' Association, so chances were a lot of the addresses were out of date. I wanted everyone on the list to be spoken to by a police officer, to be asked if they were still in touch with old classmates, if they knew any reason why they might be driven to suicide or why anyone should wish them or their ex-teachers any harm.

Thank God he didn't bring up the psychopathic old ladies again.

These days, of course, it's a lot easier to trace

people, everyone's on a computer somewhere. Back then, it took a hell of a lot longer. Most of the population didn't own a passport, half of them didn't have a driving licence or a phone in the house. We could always use the Electoral Roll, but you had to go to the town hall and look at it, not just type a name into a police computer. And then, naturally, you needed to know which town to go to. Of course, inspectors didn't do that kind of stuff, that's what constables were for, and why they needed thick soles on their boots.

I'll try and keep it short for you, save you looking at your watch too often. Took the best part of three days to track all of them down. The three women were the easiest. I don't remember their names, Felicity Shagswell, Tiffany Case and Fanny Abundant for all I know. Two were living in West Wales with their husbands, an undertaker and a solicitor. Two children each. No idea why their old school friends had topped themselves. They remembered Val Hughes quite well and reasonably fondly. The boys they hadn't been so keen on. 'Rugger Buggers' was the phrase one of them used. They hadn't done sport with Mr Jenkins, but one of them said she'd heard he was a nasty piece of work.

I got all this second hand from Half-Price. I couldn't be everywhere, and I doubted there was much they could tell us. They had no ideas about suicide pacts, and even fewer about why someone might have a grudge against their old class. Neither of them had seen any strange old ladies hanging round their houses. (Bloody Half-Price, why is it stupid people are always so determined?)

The third one, Eileen Davis…hah, looks like I did remember the name… had married a soldier and was out in Germany with him in military married quarters. One child, and the army confirmed she hadn't been back in Britain for a year. Nobody was mad keen to take a trip to Germany to find out that she knew nothing, but I eventually spoke to her on the phone. Surprise, surprise, she knew nothing, though she spoke a little more kindly of the boys in her class, maybe because her husband was a bit of a rugby man.

So, that was the five girls, Those three, Val Hughes as was and the Church Mouse. Not a clue about suicides, even less about the prospect of their being bumped off, by mad old ladies or anyone else.

So, what about the boys?

Well, we knew where three of them were…gone to their eternal rest. Haydn Lewis was easy to find, as Miss Evans had said, he was Head of Music at Tenby Grammar. I bestirred myself and DC Holt and paid him a visit.

Tallish bloke, losing his hair fairly rapidly and pretty weedy looking. 'Two pennorth o' can't help it', as my old mum might have said…not that she ever met him.

"Well indeed, Inspector, of course I heard about Councillor Hopkins, I remembered him from school. Can't say I remember him kindly, him and his rugby pals were a nasty crowd if you ask me. I got a bit of a hard time from them, not being much of a sportsman. Especially with my violin, they weren't what you'd call a cultured bunch."

Sounded like he hadn't kept in touch.

"Indeed not, I'd have crossed the street to avoid him and the others. Bowen, Probert, Herbert. Not my type at all."

I mentioned Handel Jenkins. He didn't quite spit on the staffroom floor, but I bet he wanted to. He said a word the parents of his classes might not have liked.

"I'd dance on his grave, twisted little swine. All the rugby boys worshipped him, and him them, but the rest of us he had no time for. Make your life a misery if you weren't an athlete he would, vicious tongue. It's not like I've ever needed to climb a rope or run five miles in the rain ever since. I didn't know he was dead."

Hanged himself, which was now the coroner's official word on the matter.

"Well, I won't be shedding tears. If you'd put the lever in my hand I'd have opened the trap myself."

Well, that was an interesting thing to hear. Could he account for his whereabouts etc etc. It was worth a try, but it wasn't really a serious one. He'd been nowhere near Kilgetty, and we had nobody to say any different. Still, we took a statement, and included the times of all the other deaths, just to see if he had an alibi. I think he had pretty good ones for most of them, but none at all for the Bowens. Of course, very few people do have decent alibis for anything. Mostly they're in bed, watching TV, reading a book, shopping. Perfectly reasonable things to do, but hard to prove in a court.

Didn't seem to be likely to come to that. Most of us can remember a teacher we'd have liked to murder, but very few of us decide to see them off decades later. Coming back to the suicide thing, Lewis had no ideas why some of his classmates had taken up the hobby. He certainly wasn't feeling suicidal. Perfectly happy, especially after hearing that Jenkins would be playing his rugby somewhere a bloody sight hotter from now on. His words, not mine, he was good at carrying a grudge.

So, four down and five more boys to go. Which speedily became four, once we learned that Carwyn

Herbert had driven his car off the Heads Of The Valley Road into a tree one dark and rainy night three years before. Of course, he might have done it deliberately, or one of Half-Price's old ladies might have loosened the steering. On the other hand, the Glamorgan Police suggested that the hundred percent alcohol content in his blood after a night at the local Rugby Club may have been the major factor. Anyroad, he wasn't around to be answering questions, and it seemed pointless to flog up to Brecon to talk to his widow.

Geraint Rodwell had an art studio down in Devon, which he ran with his friend Charles, according to the PC from Ilfracombe who went down to chat with him.

"An artistic type of gentleman, very brightly dressed. He claimed to have no knowledge of his former classmates, and no fond memories of St David's College, though he did speak well of Mr Pashley, the Art Master. I mentioned the names of Bowen and Hopkins and he said that they and their mates were welcome to drop dead any time."

Another one with no fond memories of the deceased, but the Devon police made a few enquiries, and he'd been down there at the time of most of the deaths. He'd been up in Tenby visiting his mother the weekend Handel Jenkins took his little jump, mind you.

That got Half-Price doing what passed for thinking again. What if he and the music bloke were in it together, maybe with that organist woman? They were all of an artistic bent (he said 'homos' actually, but I doubt your readers will stand for that). Unsurprisingly, I wasn't impressed, one nutter inducing suicides I might cope with, but three of them together? Maybe he'd just read *Murder On The Orient Express* and thought there was a conspiracy of twelve... assuming he could read.

Maybe stupidity was catching, because Veronica Holt had something on her mind too. Her old suicide watch plan.

"With all these people committing suicide, shouldn't we be keeping a close watch on the others on the list?"

And how did she propose to do that? Put a copper on every sofa to make sure they didn't swill down a bottle of pills, follow them to the seaside in case they drowned themselves?

"I just thought, we ought to offer them some kind of protection..."

Well, short of locking people in a cell and confiscating their shoelaces, there's not much protection you can offer someone against themselves. It wasn't even as if we could arrest them on suspicion of intending to commit a crime, suicide wasn't a crime anymore. Not even the oldest stupidest judge on the Welsh bench would have signed a warrant.

"But what if it isn't suicide, I mean, that's what we're thinking now, isn't it?"

That made more sense, but there was still no way we could protect all those people. The five victims were all officially suicides, we had no motive for anyone to have murdered them, or for anyone else on the list to be at risk.

"So why are we trying to trace them?"

"Copper's nose. Something's not right, but it's not something we'll sort out by putting a Panda Car outside every address on that list."

But as to what we were going to do...I still had no ideas.

Sorry, is that the time...there's my taxi. Have to go now. See you next time.

No, no...just a little visit I have to make. Can't walk with this ankle.

The first one was so easy. All I had to do was follow him for a day or two. He never noticed me, people don't expect to be followed by total strangers. Liked a drink he did, so I followed him home from the pub, crept up behind him, silent as a cat. They taught me that in the Commandos. One quick movement and he was gone.

Back again, let yourself in, the door's open. Afraid I'm a little less mobile than last time. Turns out I might have torn some ligatures or something, but I can't see the quack till next week. District nurse was due to come yesterday, but she rang up, they're shorthanded, someone called in sick. Help yourself to a drink, and pour me one. Helps to wash down the painkillers.

Yes, I know, but you've got to die of something.

Trying to track down the blokes on that list, weren't we?

John Morgan had taken over his father's farm just this side of Carmarthen. He'd lost touch with his classmates, all except Alun Watkins, who was another farmer nearby. Neither of them had any thoughts about mass suicides, neither of them held a grudge against any of their old mates nor the teachers. They'd got on all right with most of them, but being farmers' sons had plenty to do to keep them busy, so they'd not seen much of the other pupils outside school.

The last one took a little more tracking down. Gareth Hands his name was, and the people living in his mother's old house remembered that when the old lady died her son had sold the house. They thought he was a solicitor up in London.

London's a big place, so thank God his name wasn't Jones, or we'd never have found him. Actually, we never did find him, because according to the records of the Metropolitan Police, he'd thrown himself under a District Line Underground train nine months before.

He'd been number one.

We didn't go down there, his parents were dead, he'd been an only child, so there was nobody to talk to. We got the Met to send us up the transcripts of the witness reports instead. In point of fact, they didn't all agree that he'd done it deliberately. Enid Styles (age sixty from Mitcham) thought he'd stumbled as the train pulled in. Stephen Morriston (forty, Richmond) was sure he'd done it deliberately...there had been something about his face. Graham Watson (forty-eight, Hatch End) felt the crowd move forward and supposed he'd got too near the edge...and so on. The coroner had recorded an open verdict, and of course nobody had seen any need to send details to the Pembrokeshire police. Hadn't even merited a paragraph in his old hometown's newspaper.

DC Holt was all for driving down there and re-interviewing the witnesses. Might have had something to do with the fact that she'd never been to London. I had, and was hoping to be working there soon, so I didn't want to blot my copy book by stepping on the Met's toes before I even started down there. Besides, what were they going to add to what they'd said before by the time we'd driven all over Greater London and tracked them down? It wasn't as if they'd suddenly remember Half-Price's gang of murderous grannies charging up the platform waving umbrellas at the bloke.

I wanted to know a bit more about our Mr Hands mind you, but probably not about his career as a London solicitor, so I decided that perhaps a little trip to Devon might be in order. Kill three birds with one stone, find out a little bit more about the dear departed, give DC Holt a break by the sea, and take a look at another St David's Old Boy, Mr. Geraint Rodwell. Something about him had piqued my interest. Maybe it was that business of wishing his old schoolmates dead.

I can't remember if the Severn Bridge had been finished then, otherwise it might have been a bugger of a drive up through Gloucester and back down via Bristol into the West Country. Best part of a day each way. Fortunately there was a ferry from Penarth to Ilfracombe. Didn't save all that much time, but it meant a lot less driving for my little blonde chauffeuse. It was an old paddle-steamer that made the journey and it had been built long before the days of car ferries, so we boarded as foot passengers, and a PC met us in a car at Ilfracombe.

Shame we haven't got more time, or I'd give you a decent description of Penarth. Lovely little place it was, if you could afford to live there, not a patch on its pre-war heyday I was told, but even I'm not old enough to remember that.

Just pass my pills over, would you son? The blue box. Look at all this lot, if I take any more I'd rattle. Blood pressure, cholesterol, pain killers for the ankle, anti-inflagrantes for the arthritis and Viagra in case the District Nurse ever pops by. Joke, son. Except I suppose it's no joke really for us old blokes, still you lose the urge to merge by my age, so who cares whether I'm impudent or not now? Another joke...I should have been on the stage. The quack says I shouldn't be washing these tablets down with gin, so pass over that brandy bottle, will you? Ta.

Well, out from Ilfracombe we drove to a little fishing village called Woolacombe where Master Rodwell had his studio and art shop. Nice enough little village it was, long beach, bit more touristy now I dare say, but lots of artists set up there and people used to come down from miles away to look at stuff. I've no idea whether Rodwell's stuff was any good, what I saw in the shop looked pretty odd to me and pricey too, but I'm no *cornersewer* as the French say.

Rodwell looked pretty odd to me too. Dunno about pricey. The Devon PC had described him as 'an artistic type of gentleman, very brightly dressed', which seemed about right. DC Holt used the phrase 'bent as a nine-bob note', which was, of course, rather unkind of her, and you won't be printing it. Possibly not a ladies' man, is it still alright to say 'gay'? Not that he seemed exactly bright and happy, a tad waspish and bitter if you'd asked me. And I'm the only one left alive to ask, so take my word for it.

"Well, sit down Inspector, no, better not the cane chair, those cheap suits mark awfully easily, don't they? Let your little friend have that one, at the worst it'll be ninepence for some more Woolworth's stockings. A little early for the cocktail hour, so perhaps a cup of tea? Charles, would you be a dear. Sugar for you, Inspector? And you dearie? Hmmm…up to you, moment on the lips, lifetime on the hips and all that."

Yes. I quite agree, a complete stereophone…he was probably doing it for our benefit. Mostly pinched from Kenneth Williams, but it seemed to amuse him. Probably cultivated it for a bit of self-defence. Remember it was still illegal then, not that we were likely to go peeping through his windows.

"Now then my dears, how can I help you? All about my dear old school chums who seem to be dropping like flies. Good riddance to the vicious bastards I say, shame it didn't happen twenty years ago."

What, all of them?

"I suppose lots of them were pretty harmless, not exactly the most exciting bunch but then what do you expect in the middle of sheep country? The little dear with the fiddle was harmless enough, and poor Margaret. Butter wouldn't have melted in her mouth…and I daresay it never got chance to melt anywhere else either."
He laughed at that. He seemed to laugh at his own humour quite a lot. Then he lit a cigarette. He did that quite often too.

"One for you, Inspector? Turkish this side, Virginian that. No? Very wise, be the death of me. What about you dearie? Ah, a fellow slave to it. Now, come on Inspector, what's this all about? I can't believe those bastards all decided to remove themselves from a grateful world together as a public service."

Well, according to the coroner, they'd done exactly that, unless he knew different?

"I know nothing at all, we don't take the 'Shepherd's Gazette' down here. Tell me all."

So I did, I included Hands which the Devon PC wouldn't have known about.

"Hmmm…looks like all the vicious ones really have had an attack of conscience. Can't summon up a tear for any of them. Mostly the sporty chaps and girlfriends."

So he hadn't got along with any of the dear departed?

"Got along with them, Inspector? Do I look as if I'd be quaffing pints down the Rugger club with all my dear sporty chums? Made my life hell, they did. Not a day went by without some snide comment, a jogged elbow at lunch time, them putting that Hughes bitch up to blowing in my ear to try to make a fool of me. As for that nasty little gentleman Jenkins (he used a much shorter word than 'gentleman' which I dare say your paper won't be publishing) he was the most vicious sod who ever drew breath. Used to have me running laps round the rugby field for the slightest thing, but his favourites could do no wrong. Swine." Not a big fan, it seemed.

"You look like a bit of a Rugger man yourself,

Inspector. How did you use to treat the musical ones, the artistic ones, the ones who were no good at games? Big chums with them, were you? You were one of the lads. You can't really imagine what it's like to have people picking on you every day, can you?"

I was asking the questions, not answering them, so I did. He wasn't sorry to see any of them dead?

"Twenty years ago, if you'd given me a gun I'd have shot the lot of them, but now they're of no importance. Somebody said 'the best revenge is living well' and I'm quite happy down here. Hadn't given them a thought since the day I walked out of there, with a scholarship to Art School, which was a bloody sight more than most of them managed before they went off to pump petrol and muck out pigs."

I seemed to remember that he'd been back to Tenby around the time that Jenkins was hanging himself. Visiting mother, was it?

"According to that dear policeman from Ilfracombe, since I had no idea of his date of death. Yes, the old love is still going strong and always happy to see me. I even took Charles this time. 'Your butty from Devon,' she called him. You can take the girl out of the Valleys and all that. Anyway, I went nowhere near Kilgetty and I haven't got an 'Observer's Book Of Hypnotism' so I didn't pop over, dangle my dad's pocket-watch in front of him and persuade him to string himself up."

Though he did know that Jenkins lived in Kilgetty and how he'd died.

"Shouldn't you have shouted 'Aha' then, Inspector, as you cunningly tricked me into a confession? PC Bigfeet from Ilfracombe passed on the details, so I'm afraid the sweet young lady won't be able to slap the handcuffs on me just yet."

I told him about Hands then, and he pulled an exaggerated sort of face. No, I've no idea whay it meant, I always envy people who can read someone's exact mixture of emotions from a look, but not me. 'He stared at me with a mixture of contempt, lust and disappointment,' or whatever…go on, draw that face for me. Whatever expression Rodwell was wearing, it didn't seem to come with tears.

"Ha, ha, that really is quite a joke. Who'd have thought that thick sod Hands would ever have found a sense of humour."

That was beyond me, so I needed an explanation.

"Oh those joyous afternoons on the Rugger field, Inspector, some ape charging my way with the silly ball. The bastard Jenkins shouting at me to drag him down. Well, I just moved aside and let him through of course. Soon found myself running round the pitch. Not Hands though… 'Well done Hands. He'll tackle anything that boy. Tackle a bus he would'. Perhaps he should have stopped at buses, a train was obviously too much for him."

Well, now there surely were tears, and he took out a nice lilac handkerchief to wipe them away. I've rarely seen a man find anything quite so funny, callous little sod.

We stayed a little longer, but there was nothing more to be gained. His feelings towards his classmates ranged from contempt for the quiet ineffectual ones, to utter contempt for those who'd made his life harder. He had no idea, apart from a guilty conscience, what might drive them to suicide, but he had plenty of ideas about who might bear them ill-will from my list. Him, Margaret, Lewis and probably anyone else who'd ever met them.

The last steamer of the day had sailed by the time we got back to Ilfracombe, so we put up in one of the hotels there for the night. Separate rooms, of course. I didn't want Jeff Jones's eyes going through the top of his head when he saw the expenses claim.

Well, she might have, and she might not, but I'm not one to bandy a lady's name around. Separate rooms it said on the bill.

One more bloke to go, and he'd taken a while to trace. Hector Morgan his name was and he and his parents had left the area just after he'd finished at the college. His father had been a schoolmaster and had changed jobs so moved to Dinas Powys. The local Plod had gone round and discovered that Hector had qualified as a pharmacist and was running a Chemist's shop, in Broad Road, Barry. Very close to home for me, so I thought I'd combine a chat to friend Hector with a visit to friends, family and flat.

"So, will you be wanting me to drive you over to Barry, maybe stop in a hotel for the weekend?" asked DC Holt, very sweetly indeed, and no doubt in a spirit of true helpfulness.

It wouldn't be necessary, I'd drive myself on this occasion, thank you very much. I certainly wasn't feeling suicidal.

I set off on the Friday morning and got to Barry just after lunchtime. I might have mentioned that the roads were none too fast before the M4. I thought I might as well get the work part out of the way, so I picked up a DS from Barry Nick and headed up to Broad Road. His name? I dunno, son, I only used him the once. Call him Linane, he wasn't important.

So, Hector Morgan the Chemist. Medium height, medium colouring, bit of a tum on him, gold-rimmed glasses, and wearing a psychedelic kaftan. Nah, just checking you're awake, young man, oddly enough he was dressed in a white coat. He put his assistant in charge and we went into the back room.

"First I've heard of it, Inspector. I lost touch with the old class when we moved away. Decent enough bunch from what I remember. Good for sport St David's was, though I never took it any further after that. University then qualifying as a pharmacist took up all my time. Spate of suicides sounds a bit odd."

It did. It was. Could he shed any light?

"Well, no. Must be coincidence surely? Suicide isn't contagious, unless they were all being blackmailed for some dark secret in their past? Cheating in a Maths exam?"

Nobody laughed, though the blackmail idea was one that hadn't come up before. Might even have made sense. Blackmail victims quite often take a desperate way out, in books at any rate. I mentioned the names of the deceased.

"Decent enough crowd from what I remember, lively bunch we were, mostly. Couple of quiet ones, of course."

What did he remember of the quiet ones.

"Couple of musicians... Haydn Evans? Margaret Lewis, I remember. Poor kid, not much of a looker. One of the God Squad, I think. Then there was our resident fairy, Geraint Rodwell. Perhaps quiet wasn't the right word for him, always had plenty to say for himself. Very arty-farty if you know what I mean."

So they'd have had a hard time at school, fair bit of bullying?

"Oh no, nothing like that. Bit of leg-pulling I suppose, few nicknames and all that. But nothing malicious. All good-humoured. I'm sure they took it in the right spirit, no hard feelings, just kids, eh?"

Well, he seemed pretty sure of it, one or two others we'd spoken to had different views. Could they have held a grudge all this time?

"No, surely. People grow up, it was just kids' banter, happens in every school, nobody takes any notice. Anyway, what would it matter now, you said suicides."

Yes, I had, hadn't I, because that's what the might of the law said. Did Mr Morgan have any suicidal tendencies? How was business?

"Very good actually, in fact I'm negotiating to open another shop, up in Cadoxton. Get someone else in to run it of course. No, Inspector, I don't see any chance of me joining in any suicide pact. Business is good, I'm happily married, two children and no health problems... touch wood."

You're probably getting as bored with it as I was, same questions, same answers, and even after discovering the link, we didn't seem to be much further forward. It was either a statistical anemone, or we had the cleverest killer since Jack The Ripper doing away with people on the basis of the school they'd attended.

That was my duty in Barry done, so perhaps it was time to test that 'all work and no play' thing and see what I could find to amuse myself for the weekend. Well, the what was pretty obvious, just a question of the who. I went back to my flat, blew the dust off my phone and address book and made a call. Alright, I didn't need the address book, I knew WPC Jane Langdon's number well enough. Barry 2747 since you didn't ask.

"Oh, you're still alive are you? Thought you must be dead, or all the phones in Tenby out of order, are they?"

It had only been a week or so since I'd phoned. Alright, maybe two, but I'd been busy running round all over the place.

"Running round after some Tenby girls, more like it. I know all about you."

She had to be bluffing, she couldn't have known anything about it. I laughed it off. Anyway, I was back in Barry for the weekend, so how about...

"Well, you're not the only one who gets busy now and then. I'm on nights finishing tonight as it happens. I might be free tomorrow night, if nothing else comes up."

I said I'd pick her up at seven, and we'd go to the pictures.

"Oh, there's sophisticated. I'll see if I can find 3/6 to

buy my own ticket shall I? I suppose I'll have to pay for the ice-creams too."

I gave up then and said I'd see her tomorrow. I've never been fond of sarky women, which is a shame, as I've never seemed to meet any other sort. Talking of which, or is it whom, I decided that duty called, so I spent Friday night visiting my mum. She had a few points to make about my behaviour, manners, dress sense and diction. None of them complimentary. Fortunately she shut up when Michael Miles came on the telly, and devoted some time to shouting 'open the box' at a few contestants. Good show that was.

I'll speed over the rest of the weekend. I took Jane to the Tivoli to see some Elvis film. She loved Elvis, I didn't mind him when he was singing but his films had got bloody awful by then. She stopped being sniffy long enough to come back to my place for a little drink and to check that her pill was still working.

"Well, good to see there's one thing you haven't forgotten how to do, Inspector Williams. Been keeping your hand in over there, have you?"
I wasn't the blushing type, but I was bloody glad it was dark.

Sunday lunchtime, I started back to Tenby. Gave me the perfect excuse to miss Mother's cooking.

There's the taxi again, see yourself out will you? Just need to pop to the little boy's room.

Well, actually it is being nosey, but I'll tell you

anyway. I'm going to visit my wife. She's in a home, has been for two months. Doesn't even recognise me now, so I can't honestly tell you why I bother going. Except that she's my wife. Alzheimer's they call it. Funny, it's about the only long word I never make a mistake on.

Yes. I'm bloody sorry about it too.

Be seeing you.

Hello again, door's open…I'm no more mobile than last time, can get about indoors with the stick. Help yourself, and pour me one too.

Tenby again, then? Things had come to such a pretty pass that I was almost inclined to give one of Half-Price's theories a try. No, not the one about the cyclepathic old ladies, but perhaps the one about three of them being in it together. The three artistic ones. Don't ask me why, desperation does strange things to a policeman. Or did, haven't been one for a bloody long time, have I?

I decided to try Haydn Lewis again since he was the nearest, but he wasn't home. Neighbour said he'd gone on holiday to Anglesey. What in God's name possessed someone who lived by the sea in West Wales to flog all the way up North for worse weather amongst the bloody North Welsh? Odd people up there, I tell you. Sea's full of jellyfish too. That was where he was and it didn't seem worth looking for him at the time. So, Miss Church Mouse it was, but this time I waited till she got home from the bank. Took Half-Price this time, I didn't need any more sark from young Veronica.

"Inspector Williams. How nice to see you again. Come through into the front room, Mum, dad, it's Inspector Williams. Probably about the Reverend Probert again. I'll ask him, would you like a cup of tea, Inspector? Yes please, mum. Two. Milk no sugar. Now come in and sit down Inspector. Sergeant Price. I'd rather you didn't smoke, my father's chest is bad."

It was time I got a word in, so I told her I didn't smoke, then I told her about Hands. That stopped the flow for a moment or two.

"Gareth Hands too? When? Oh that's awful. I mean I was never a great friend of his, but still. What's that now…five suicides? Six with Mr Jenkins. How did it happen?"

I gave her a few details, then asked how well she remembered him.

"Well, I remember him, of course, though as I say we weren't really friends. He didn't have any interest in music…or in me."

She stopped then. Seemed to be thinking.

"Truth to tell, Inspector, none of the boys in the class had much interest in me. I was a dowdy little thing then. Still am I suppose."

I tried to think of something to say, but it didn't come out convincingly.

"It's alright, Inspector. I've got a mirror, and it hasn't told me anything nice since I started looking at it. I was never going to be a Marian Monroe. Most of the girls were kind enough to me, and the boys just pretty much ignored me, unless hey wanted some help with their maths homework. Except Michael Hopkins, he could be cruel when he wanted to. He'd say things like 'You're looking lovely today, Maggie, perhaps I should ask for a date,' and then I'd hear him laughing with his pals. He gave up on it after a bit, started paying more attention to the girls in the Lower Sixth. One after the other. I think a couple of the other girls told him off too."

I mentioned another couple of people who'd been given a hard time by the rugby crowd.

"Haydn, yes he was always a bit quiet and wound up in his music. Bit like me, I suppose. He took me to the pictures a couple of times, but his heart wasn't in it. Nor mine, come to that, but he was pleasant enough company. I think he'd had a harder time lower down the school, but most of the boys had grown out of it by the end. We had plenty of friends amongst the other musicians, the school was nearly as proud of its orchestra as its sports teams. It pretty much settled down as we got older. Bowen and Hands were probably the worst. Natural bullies. Aneurin Probert was no saint either, but he changed completely when he came back. Gentle as a lamb he was."

Geraint Rodwell?

"Well, he was definitely different. Lived for his art, he did, but very bright at other subjects too. Lots of sniggering behind his back... used to keep his hair a bit longer than most. I don't think they kept on at him as much though, he had a vicious tongue on him. He wasn't a weakling either, though he hated sports. Nobody ever tried it on with him. I don't think Mr Jenkins liked him at all from what I heard, but of course us girls hardly ever saw him."

I asked about the other two. Could they still be

nursing some sort of grudge?

"Oh no, it was all so long ago, and 'boys will be boys' as they used to say. Not a very nice bunch some of them, and I don't miss them, but I'm sure Haydn and Geraint would have forgotten about them long ago. Anyway, neither of them ever had it as bad as poor little Quentin."

What? Who the bloody hell was Quentin? No bugger had mentioned any Quentin, why wasn't he on the list?

"Oh well, he wouldn't be would he, 'cause he was never in the leaving class. Left at the end of the Lower Sixth he did. Poor little devil, he had a rotten time."

…and nobody had thought to mention him? Tell me all, Miss Evans.

"Quentin Passmore his name was…funny little bloke. His father was dead and his mother had married again, so she had a different name I think. I think he was a bit younger than the rest of us, been bumped up a year since he was very bright. Short, fat with thick glasses. No good at games and a bit of a swot, so he was always getting picked on. His name made it worse, I think his middle name was Stephen, so they used to call him Spazmore…or just Spaz. Horrible to him they were, poor little soul. Most of the girls felt sorry for him, he was just a little kid amongst all those teenagers. Well, not that they'd invented the word then, but they were practically men. I remember once three or four of them took his trousers off and threw them over the rugby crossbar. Poor love was in tears…I think one of the farmers fetched them down for him, Alun Watkins."

And why not mention this before?

"Well, you were talking about the leaving class, so I concentrated on that and he was never in it. I'd almost forgotten about him till I thought about it now. He wasn't exactly a strong character, poor love. And then he left."

Left for where?

"I'm not sure really. He just didn't come back for the last September. I did hear his stepfather died and he went abroad with his mother somewhere, I dunno New Zealand, South Africa or somewhere. Lots of people emigrated in those days. We weren't friends really, so he never told me anything, maybe his mother organised it all quickly. Poor little soul, fancy going through your life being called 'Spaz'."

Well, I know it's not PC, young man, but that doesn't change history. Daresay there might be people these days who don't know why it came to be a term of abuse. Short for 'spastic', which nobody uses now, though it used to be the accepted medical term. The charity was called The Spastics Society, though it long ago changed its name to 'Vision' or 'Aspire' or something. Brian Rix used to do a lot of work for it, his son was one I think. Actor he was, long time ago. Spastic, if you look it up in the dictionary it'll tell you that its an offensive term for someone 'afflicted with cerebral palsy'. I know, I looked it up this morning.

You know, one of those poor sods who can't seem to control their limbs and have all kinds of problems talking. No idea if they abort most of then now, but you still see a few. Generally in short buses, being taken to the seaside. Used to have a friend whose uncle was one. Nice guy, had a printing press in his garden shed. Used to do wedding invites and stuff, it was odd to watch him setting up the type when he could hardly stop his hands shaking. No fool either, though you needed practice to make out what he was saying. Uncle Stan the spastic.

I believe even 'cerebral palsy' is out these days. They tend to say 'learning difficulties'. Fine PC phrase, but makes no bloody sense to me. Makes it sound like they're not too good at maths, or just failed their history exam, rather than can't control the way they walk and talk.

Odd how people are always changing the names of things they feel uncomfortable with. Nobody ever mentions 'abortion' now, it's always 'Choice' or 'Planned Parenthood', or 'Life' if you're on the other side of the argument. Nobody in Britain can ever be described as Pakistani or Indian it has to be 'Asian'. Prostitutes are now 'workers in the sex industry'. Soon you won't be allowed to say 'murder', it'll be 'involuntary demise' and rape will be 'a non-consensual sexual experience'.

Still, I bet kids don't shout 'learning difficulty' at some chubby guy with glasses who can't play football and gets 'accidentally' knocked over every playtime.

Yes, well I'm sorry about it and sorry about his name, but I don't see how you can change it without the thing making no sense. Passmore was his name, known to his detractors as Spaz. Like it or not.

So it seemed that Passmore would have had more of a grudge against some of his old classmates than anyone, yet nobody'd thought to mention him to us. Probably just because we hadn't asked. I called Tenby Nick and got them to get started on a search for him. The College might be a good place to phone for his last known address. By the time I got back there myself, they had an address and DC Holt had gone round to see what might come of it. It seems their records just showed that he'd left the school, rather than where he went. Useless buggers.

Me, I called Geraint Rodwell in Woolacombe. I had neither the time nor the inclination for another day out there and the phone was quicker and easier on my nerves.

"Ooh, Inspector, how lovely to hear from you. You're not coming down with your lady friend and her handcuffs are you?"

I told him to turn it up, I didn't have time to play Julian and Sandy today. I wanted to know about Quentin Passmore.

"Poor little Spaz? Heavens, I'd quite forgotten about him. Left at the end of the Lower Sixth. Yes... now there was a chap who had a hard time from the cavemen. Just a little chubby kid really, clumsy but musical. No harm in him, but they gave him the hell of a time."

Any special reason, anyone in particular?

"The usual vicious crowd, and probably just because he was different and vermin like that always hate anything different. Just between you, me and the bedpost, Inspector, I think he might have been a little bit queer you know, though he probably hadn't realised it. Some don't till later. Now me, I was fancying the doctor in the delivery room, but some fight it. I think he was. And being young, chubby and that stupid name, he was such an easy target. If I hadn't been so busy looking after myself, I'd have felt sorry for him."

But what happened to him? Where did he go?

"Maybe he begged his parents to take him away. I would have if I'd had his life. All I know is that he was there in July and never came back in September. Sadly I don't think too many people cared. I have the feeling he moved away. But I really couldn't say where."

Nor could anybody else from his class, we asked all the survivors. Vague talk of Canada or maybe Australia, but nobody knew for sure. It seemed nobody had been friendly enough with the poor little bugger to take much interest. Looked like we might have to do it the hard way.

It definitely looked even more that way when DC Holt got back from her enquiries. The house in Tenby that was Passmore's last-known address had been sold a few times in the intervening years and the present occupants had no knowledge of him and his family. Not being stupid, she'd asked quite a few of the neighbours, but drawn a blank. Seaside towns are always full of old people, so the turnover can be a bit rapid. Just like here in Eastbourne. God's waiting room, they call it. My number'll be coming up soon I dare say. Jane's pretty much has, poor love.

So, it was going to be the very hard way. If only we'd had all those computers I could have found him in ten minutes. Probably my grandson could have on his Eye-Pad thing. But no, it was going to take a long time.

Well, we had a good idea of the date in question, so the first thing to do was to see if Quentin Stanley Passmore had been issued with a passport around that time. Since he would only have been sixteen, he might have been on his mother's or stepfather's passport instead. Of course, the whole family might have held passports from years before. If we could find the application, then we might have a chance of learning where they'd gone, since they used to ask you for your destination and expected date of travel on the application form.

Some constable was told off to get on to the Passport Office in Petty France. No doubt they started blowing the cobwebs off their records from all those years ago, and we'd get an answer when they found one. At least there weren't likely to be many people answering to the name of Quentin Stanley Passmore, which was more than could be said for his parents, Sheila and John Jones. We'd got that at least from the College records. Somebody'd mentioned that Passmore's father had died and his mother had remarried. Shame for the poor little sod's sake that she hadn't changed his name to Jones as well.

I assumed he'd have needed a visa of some sort for most countries, so the next set of phone calls were to the various Emabassies, Consulates or High Commissions, whatever they were called. New Zealand, Australia, Canada, South Africa, Rhodesia, all the popular Commonwealth countries. There'd been a lot of migration around then, but they were the main choices. I supposed we might have tried Kenya, Hong Kong and so on later. We'd be needing to wait while they searched through dusty files too.

I didn't have a lot of manpower to play with, but I sent a couple of constables round the neighbourhood to try a more intensive search for somebody who remembered Mrs Jones, her second husband and her unrepossessing son. Maybe someone could remember the bloke's job, any other relatives. It was a fairly long shot, but it had to be tried.

As old Superintendent Watkins used to say, far too often,

"Williams, you'll catch ninety-nine criminals by routine investigation for every one that's the result of inspiration."

It's why real police work doesn't make good books or drama, it takes a long time and it's mostly very dull. And the guilty party is almost never a member of the investigating officer's social circle. Bloody

Hell, I've read a book lately where the murderer actually worked in the Nick, cataloguing items of evidence, and one where it was the DS's brother who just happened to be the mystery drug addict lopping off heads all over town. Load of cock, son, but it sells. That's why the *Daily Mail* turned down my memoirs, not enough excitement, and the murderer quite often turned out to be a total stranger to the detective. That's probably why your mob will turn me down too, Dunno why you keep showing up to listen to an old fart ramble on.

Still, since you're here, help yourself to another drink. It's all my shout now, but I've got bugger all else to spend my pension on. And fill mine up and all.

Asking the neighbours turned out to be a dead duck, maybe the Jones family hadn't made many friends, maybe they'd all moved, maybe asking about people called Jones in Wales is a waste of time.

The information that helped came from two different sources, and within ten minutes of each other, as it turned out.

The Passport Office had issued a passport in the name of Quentin Stanley Passmore on the fourth of June that particular year. The form had been filled in by his mother, Sheila Grace Jones, formerly Passmore née Jones and the photo was countersigned by Doctor Charles Williams of the Saundersfoot Surgery.

Yes, Williams, same as me, there's plenty of us about. And she'd started off as Jones, married a Passmore then re-married and became Jones again. Well, it happens. If it confuses your readers make her maiden name Windsor or Thatcher or something.

The planned destination on the passport was Melbourne, Australia with the date of travel given as the second of September that same year.

Ten minutes later came another call, this time from Australia House. Residence and work visas had been granted to Dr Sheila Grace Jones and Dr Henry William Jones in August that year, accompanied by the son of her first marriage, Quentin Stanley Passmore. None of your ten quid immigration passages though, they'd both been sponsored by the Royal Victorian Hospital. Melbourne.

Bingo.

DC Holt got quite excited by that idea, she'd missed out on a trip to London, but she saw the chance of something much more exciting in prospect. No hope, there was bugger-all chance of anyone sanctioning trips Down Under to try to find out why a few people had done themselves in unexpectedly. And it wasn't as if we had any evidence of Passmore or his parents having done anything. Still, as they used to say on the telly, we'd started so we were bloody well going to finish. But no visits, though I did get to Melbourne later on when I was working in the Met, but that's a much duller story.

We did it via expensive phone calls. Might have been cheaper to send someone out there. Course, we had to call at stupid times, otherwise they'd all have been asleep. I put my two eager bloodhounds on it, the lovely Veronica and Half-Price. I think somebody wound him up that he'd need an interpreter since he didn't speak Australian. He claimed he never believed it, but I had my doubts.

Still, Half-Price might not have been the brightest penny in the pile, but you couldn't fault his determination. It was about three days later that he walked into my office looking like the cat who'd got the cream.

"I've traced him Inspector Williams, traced him for sure. But it looks like it's nothing to do with him at all."

And why not?
"Well, first of all he moved to Melbourne in Australia all those years ago, second of all there's no trace of him ever returning or even getting his passport renewed. And third of all, he's been dead sixteen years."

God grant me strength and patience.

"You know, Price, if that had been me I'd probably have put number three first. It sorts of renders the first two slightly irreverent."

"Perhaps, Inspector, But I was just presenting the information in the order I received it."

Never argue with the stupid, they'll drag you down to their level and beat you with experience. Yes, wise words indeed, young man. Oscar Wilde probably, or Mark Twain, they said most things between them.

I just confined myself to asking whether the Australian authorities had managed to inform him of the cause of young Passmore's demise.

"'Anged 'imself apparently, Sir. Only eighteen he was an' all."

Jesus Thomas, not another one. What the bloody hell had been going on at that school?

The details were sketchy, young Passmore had certainly hanged himself and an Aussie coroner had called it suicide. No note, but no suspicious circumstances. His mother and step-father had moved from Melbourne and it seemed pointless to try tracing them, since we didn't have any intelligent questions about their son's death to ask them.

We were back to square one.

And square one is where that enquiry officially ended. We had seven suicides, or it looked that way. The connection with St David's College made it a huge coincidence, but that was all we had. We couldn't find one suspect or really even say that we had a sniff of a case of murder anywhere. We'd tried everything, even trying to fit together a jigsaw that would make Half-Price's theory of a wimp's conspiracy work, but there was no hope.

Jeff Jones called me in.

"Williams, it's case closed on this one I'm afraid. I can't think of anything you could have done differently and it's no reflection on you. It's the oddest thing I've come across in many long years, but it seems that odd is all it is. The Met want you down in London next week, so that's it as far as we're concerned. I'll be writing a report for Glamorgan, and you can be sure it'll speak of you in very positive terms. In the end we just gave you a case where there wasn't a case."

There was nothing I could say to that, we'd looked under every stone and found nothing. He offered me the services of DC Holt to drive me back to Barry Nick, but I decided to take the train. I'd seen enough suicides lately, and I wasn't going to risk Jane Langdon's temper. I saw Veronica before I left though.

"Well, it's been nice knowing you, Inspector. Off up the big city now I hear. Good luck with that."

"Same to you DC Holt, hope you keep busy."

"Might well do, my young man's discharge is due soon."

We didn't meet again, though I used to get Christmas cards. They stopped about ten years ago.

Anyway, young man, that was the official end of the Saundersfoot Suicides enquiry. There were never any more, and it remained a statistical anemone.

And there's my taxi.

Nah, I wouldn't leave you like that. Pop back next week, and I might have something interesting to tell you.

Just one more left, and he was no problem. Funny how all those big tough swine from school looked so much smaller, once you knew how to deal with them. He was no match for me, never even knew what   hit   him.

So, they'd tried to ruin my life, but ended up ruining their own. I had the whole of mine ahead of me, and some choices to make. First, I'd be needing a job, which should be no problem for somebody with my military record. Then maybe time to settle down, a wife and children. And I'd make bloody sure no kid of mine was ever bullied. It was done now, and I could finally move forward. Life was going to be good.

Theirs was over, mine was just beginning.

Well now, if you're listening to this, Mr James or maybe even Mz Turnbull, it's because I'm dead. Hope you've found a cassette machine to play it on, and I'm sorry about the poor quality. Ha, we could call it my Crap Last Tape, except someone else got there before me with that title. Becket, I think. Williams's last attempt at a joke anyway.

You probably think it's a little sudden me cashing in my chips, but I've been thinking about it for a while. Some of those aches and pains I've been developing seem a little more serious than before, and I really can't be arsed letting the quack dice and slice me to get a few more months.

Jane's been the main thing, seeing her go like that broke my heart, and I just couldn't keep on visiting someone who had no idea who I was, or even who she was. She wouldn't have wanted to end up like that, sat in a chair all day, having to be fed, taken to the toilet. It was a relief when she died on Monday.

As for me, what's left? My time's done, I'm an old fool in a world that doesn't need or want me anymore and which I understand less every day. It seems like all the things I'd been brought up to believe in have changed so much that I'm a bigot for sticking to them. Well, the young people will have one less dinosaur to throw abuse at now.

Still, wouldn't have been fair to leave you on tenterloins after all this time, would it? And I bet you've got no more ideas than the rest of them. I'm bloody sure it'll never make the *Telegraph*. Far too long and slow. Maybe there's a book in it mind, not that anyone would ever believe it. You could give it a try though.

Well, let's play fair with you.

I found out about it something like two years later. I'd been doing well in the Met, saved enough to set myself up down in London and got round to proposing to Jane. We'd had some idea of her applying for a transfer, but in the end she decided she could live without ever dressing up in blue serge again and she quit the force. We were going to get married in Barry in the June and we were up there to pick bridesmaids' dresses. We had the usual, the skinny one, the fat one and the kid, so we had to pick a style and colour that looked wrong on all of them. It's apparently a humiliation that all women have to go through.

I didn't use to get back to Barry much, and I was noticing a few changes. We drove down to Broad Road where the bridal shop was, and I noticed that Morgan's Chemist now bore the name of Slade's Chemist. He'd seemed a bit young to retire.

Jane knew nothing about it, so I left her to choose between mauve, lilac and some vile shade of green and popped down the road.

I suspect they must issue all chemists with thinning hair, white coats and gold-rimmed glasses and I'd have been hard put to tell this one from Morgan in an identity parade, though he might have been a little taller and younger. I showed him the warrant card and asked him how long he'd been in the shop.

"It seems a little strange for a Metropolitan Police officer to be in Barry asking questions, Chief Inspector?"

No fool, he. Well, really I'd just shown him the warrant card for the sake of form, I'd known the previous proprietor Mr Morgan, and I was just wondering what had become of him. No investigation or anything.

"He died, Chief Inspector. Quite suddenly in fact, about a year ago."

Well now. there's a thing. Any idea how he'd died?

"Yes, a massive heart attack apparently. Dropped dead here in the shop I heard. I was running his Cadoxton branch at the time, so I bought the business out from his wife. Widow. Well, the bank and I bought it."

And how was business?

"Going very well, he'd built it up successfully, and nobody seems to think the place might be haunted. Terrible shame, he was no age."

We agreed that it came to us all and fate played strange tricks. I wondered if he remembered the exact date?

"I do indeed, the eighteenth of April. It's not every day your boss drops dead."

I tended to agree.

Jane was meeting her mother that afternoon to decide how many carrots to put on each guest's plate or something equally vital, so I was at a loose end. I amused myself by popping into the main library in King's Square and having a browse through some old copies of the *Barry And District News.* Interestingly enough, I picked some from April of the previous year.

The story was there right enough. Howard Morgan a well-known local businessman had died in his shop in Broad Street, leaving a wife and two children. A doctor had been on the scene pretty quickly, followed by an ambulance, but all efforts to revive him failed and he'd been pronounced dead at Barry General.

I read on a few weeks, but there was no mention of an inquest, so I assume it must have been cut and dried. But as I say, I had nothing to do, so I thought I'd stick my copper's nose in a bit. From the story in the paper, it was doubtful that the boys in blue would have been involved, so I wandered round some doctors' surgeries.

The third one had a receptionist who remembered the case very well.

"Oh yes, poor Mr Morgan. He was actually a patient of ours, and Dr Cooper was walking past on her way to another patient when she heard him cry out. She went in and did whatever, but it was no use. Dead when he hit the floor apparently."

Might as well have a word with Dr Cooper.

"No, she doesn't work at the surgery, she was just doing some locum work for us at the time while Dr McGill was off having her second. Nice lady. I believe she's retired now."

Might they have an address for the nice lady?

"Oh yes, well seeing as it's the police. Here you are, Dr Grace Cooper, nice little flat over on Cold Knap."

I thought about phoning first, I thought about having a word with Dai Watkins and seeing if he'd lend me a DS.

In the end, I just drove over to see if she was in.

Dry work all this talking, you'll probably guess what I'm drinking now, young man. Not many more to go.

She was in. Nice looking woman indeed, though she wouldn't be seeing sixty again. Plenty of rich brown hair, but I doubted it was natural. Very bright blue eyes. Still wore full make-up and a smart green suit. I wondered for a bit who she reminded me of, and I thought maybe an older version of Mrs Bowen, though I'd only seen her dead and in pictures. She looked puzzled when she answered the door. She looked even more puzzled when I showed her the Warrant Card.

"A London policeman? Come in Chief Inspector, though I guess with that accent you're no cockney."

Nor was she, I'd have said Cardiff originally, though been around.

"Too right I have. Now, what can I do for you?"

But it was too late, I'd got it. I'd probably never have got it from the face, it's amazing the difference women can make to themselves, but that one little phrase gave her away.

"Well, for a start, you can tell me why the last time I met you, you were calling yourself Edna Perkins and cleaning the Bowens' house for them."

She laughed, which I wasn't expecting at all, then went and sat on the sofa.

"I was wondering how long it might take you to spot me. I knew I was done the moment I opened the door. Cigarette? No? I don't either, but Edna did of course. That was hard work starting, and hard work giving up again afterwards. Sometimes I even miss the dear old stick."

I was stunned. I'd come expecting to confirm a natural death and here was the whole thing opening up before me again. So who was she really?

"Grace Cooper is correct, Inspector Williams… sorry, Chief Inspector now, is it? It's remarkably hard to practise medicine in most countries under a false name."

"It wouldn't be 'Sheila Grace Cooper' by any

chance, would it?"

"Indeed it would, but when I moved to Australia, I decided that the country didn't need any more Sheilas, so I swapped over. My late husband never got used to it."

Mr Jones was deceased then? Dr Jones, begging his pardon. Surely not...

"Lung cancer, Inspector. Nasty way to go, he was a smoker and they say that causes it. While we're on the subject, Mr Cooper was a stroke. Dropped dead in a bar in Sydney. They say heavy drinking can cause that, and he certainly put it away. Which reminds me, where are my manners? Whisky? Gin? Tea?"

You'll be surprised to learn that I turned them all down. Didn't seem advisable in the circumstances. I asked after the late Mr Passmore.
"You did do your homework. Must have got quite close then. No, I'm sorry to say I was never entitled to the title of Mrs Passmore. I was a fallen woman Mr Williams, in my junior doctor days. Didn't have the pill back then, and the head of surgery was a little careless. A little married too. I took myself off somewhere they didn't know me after Quentin was born and took his name for a while. They didn't ask to see marriage certificates when you registered a birth. Told Quentin his dad had died in the war. First big mistake. Poor little bugger."

"Well then, Dr Cooper, do I ask questions, do we go down to the station, or do you just tell me all about it?"

"Bit clichéd that, isn't it, Mr Williams? The evil scheming villainess pours out the whole story to the baffled detective? Shouldn't I be holding you at gunpoint?"

Well, there had been the threat of the whisky.

She laughed again, a bit longer this time.

"Bless you, you're quite safe with me. I've done all I needed to now. It won't matter for much longer anyway."

"Why not tell me about Quentin?"

"My kid, Mr Williams. All I had for a while, and I loved him fiercely. Then I married. Ray Jones was a good man, he treated Quentin well, but he wanted kids of his own, and we couldn't. Maybe the disappointment took my focus off Quentin and I didn't see some things I should have. I was all he had in the world, and I let him down so badly. And I never knew."

The school?

"I never knew any of it. His reports were good, well except PE, and he was such a bright kid, I really thought it was fine. Every time I asked about school he'd have good news about English or Chemistry, and he never mentioned the bullying, the name calling. When we emigrated, I reckon it must have got worse, Australian kids could be rough if you didn't muck in. But still he never said anything, never once. And then after six months we found him hanging from his bedroom door."

I must have said something, but I don't remember what.

"It broke my heart. I'd failed him. He was a funny little soul, but he was my funny little soul, and now I'd lost him and never knew why. For months I couldn't go into his room. Could barely manage to drag myself into work. Eventually Ray got a move to Sydney and it was easy for me to find a job there too. Ray packed up all Quentin's stuff for me...I couldn't bear to look at it. But I couldn't bear to throw it out either. Three boxes of it in our attic in Sydney all those years. After Ray died, I married a colleague, Colin Cooper a few years later. Not love's young dream, but we were company for each other, and he moved into my place. I didn't have long with him, and when he went I decided I'd done with Australia. I wanted to finish off in the Land Of My Fathers."

No accounting for taste, young man. I'd have stuck to Australia. So I assumed she sold up?

"That's right, and I finally got rid of poor Quentin's stuff. That's when I found his book."

He'd kept a diary?

"No, it was more than that. He'd written a little book, he was always good at English. A book, with his life the way he wanted it to be. Up until he was sixteen or so, it was his own story, and that's where I found out about all the bullying, the name-calling. Not just kids but teachers too. The hell he'd been through."

There were tears in her eyes, and she reached for a cigarette, stopped herself, then took one anyway.

"No, that's not me, is it. Still, why not, one last one for Edna. School. The bastards had made his life a misery, driven him desperate. So he wrote his own happy ending."

I didn't understand, but she went on.

"In his book, he toughened up, found a girlfriend and then went off to Cambridge to study chemistry. After that he joined the army, the commandos. Went up to captain in no time. Then he left, and came back home to a place where nobody recognised him, he was taller, fitter, wore a moustache. And he started revenging himself on the people who'd been so vicious to him as a kid. He could kill silently, he knew all about untraceable poisons. And he finished all the bastards off. It was a good read, but none of it ever happened."

"You're telling me you made it happen all these years later? But that's completely insane. You're a doctor, not a murderer."

"It seems you can mix the two, Inspector. And I think you're right...I must be insane. I read that book of his over and over again, especially the first part, and I think knowing how he'd suffered, knowing the way those swine treated him, deprived him of his life, how they took my son from me... Insane's probably right. I swore to do what he hadn't been able to. Kill the bastards."

Well. I may have mentioned the futility of arguing with the stupid, it also seemed pointless arguing with the fixated. Especially once the fixation had been carried out. What was I meant to say? It made no sense, but it had to her.

Now in five minutes, I'd learned who and I knew why, but I still needed to know how. Though, once you knew who, the how began to get a bit clearer. Hands must have been easy.

"Oh yes. It's not hard to find people if you can gossip a bit, and know where to start looking. Once I knew he was a solicitor in London, he was easy enough to track down. I took a little locum work there and followed him for a few days. He never even looked at me. Why would he? It's the invisibility of the old lady, you see. Nobody takes any notice of us, and the dowdier you look the more invisible you become."

Dear God, I swore that Half-Price would never get to hear of this, he'd been right all along. So just a quick push on a crowded platform.

"That's right, as much to see if I could as anything else. And I could. I even gave a nice statement to the police."

But that was just the dress-rehearsal for the trip to West Wales? That would be much more dangerous.

"I thought it might be, I thought people might recognise me, but nobody ever did. Quite a difference between young Mrs Jones from all those years ago and Edna Perkins. No make up, curlers and scarf, housecoat and cigarette. That's all anyone ever saw. People don't look at faces all that much."

Char for the Bowens, how could that happen?

"The purest luck. I was going to poison their milk on the doorstep, but I heard they were looking for a daily and got the job. It was an amazing coincidence, but it only made things slightly easier. I poisoned the open tonic water bottle when I went round there. Next day I pitched up as usual, opened a different bottle and poured a little away, put my nicotine bottle in his pocket, washed up the poisoned tonic bottle and threw it in next door's bin when I went to phone. I was surprised to get both, I don't know if they used to toast each other and then take a good swig. It was him I really wanted...if I'd got him I don't think I'd have gone back for her. But if one of them had survived, you'd have caught me for sure. Lucky, I guess."

And we'd have rumbled her in five minutes if we'd only known who she bloody was. Once you know where to look, the answer was obvious. His Reverence must have been similar.

"Not quite. I just walked up to his front door and knocked. He was always pleased to see a parishioner with a problem and we had a cup of tea.

His ended up with quite a few sleeping pills in it, and then I poured a little whisky into him. Had to pull him into the kitchen. I even thought about a cushion for him. Shame, he was a nice man in the end, but it didn't alter what he'd been."

I'll tell you, whoever's listening, I've talked to some cold-blooded murderers in my time, but never anyone who discussed it as matter-of-fact as that women. She might have been talking about baking a cake rather than gassing a parson.

"Hopkins I rather enjoyed, he seemed a very nasty piece of work. He never bothered locking his garage when he was out, so I thought about hiding inside, but in the end I just popped up his drive and hung around by the side around the time the pubs closed. He hadn't been to a pub I found out later, but it was much the same time. He opened the doors, pulled inside, opened the car door, I ran in and put a pad of chloroform over his face. It acts very quickly. Turned the car engine back on, shut the door and then left pretty sharpish."

But a big bloke like that? What if he'd hit her?

"I wasn't exactly a weak old woman, Chief Inspector. People in Australia spend a lot of time outdoors and I'd liked swimming and tennis, so I was stronger than I looked back then. It was mostly surprise, of course, who expects an old lady to attack them? He was plastered too, could barely walk, so by the time he knew what was happening it was done. Could have gone wrong, but, you see, I didn't really care."

Jesus, she scared me. Ruthless and so inventive. And, as she'd said, invisible. But how had she persuaded Jenkins to hang himself?

"Oh I didn't. I turned up at his house with a tin and some lifeboat flags and sold him one. Then I asked for a drink of water. When his back was turned I broke his neck."

She did what?

"It was Quentin's commando stuff that gave me the idea. As a doctor I knew how vulnerable the neck was, and it wasn't hard to find some self-defence books. I talked to a few Anzacs bck in Sydney too, they were happy to show me stuff. Maybe thought I was kinky or something. He was very small, old and weak, and it only takes one quick determined jerk from behind. I was surprised how simple it was, I hadn't been able to practise, of course. I could show you, if you like?"

You won't be surprised to hear that I declined that offer too. I couldn't believe it…a sixty year old Emma Peel dealing out death with her bare hands? You wouldn't read about it, but I asked some people afterwards and they said it was perfectly possible. Sort of thing they really did teach you in the army.

"Though I really should have tried to lure him upstairs first. It took a very long time to drag him up, tie the noose and throw him over the banister. I was worried someone might ring the doorbell. Then I just left. Nobody was about."

And around that time, Edna Perkins went off to visit her poorly sister in Ponty? And we forgot all about her.

"I was sure I said Glyneath...but then who listens to silly old ladies? I'd done what I needed to do, so Edna disappeared and I turned back into Dr Cooper and went looking for some locum work over here. It's a nice spot, I almost thought of settling down, but I had one more bastard to dispose of."

But the man had a wife and kids? Had she no pity?

"What about my Quentin's wife and kids? He never had the bloody chance because of those swine."

I didn't bother repeating Rodwell's assessment of Quentin's prospects in that direction. I assumed that Morgan hadn't died of a heart attack.

"Oh, but he did, that's the beauty of it. I walked into his shop and shoved a needle into him. Full of Potassium Chlorate."

I think that's what she said, I tried looking it up afterwards, but didn't find out much. Never thought to Joogle it now.

"Stops the heart almost straight away. He only cried out the once."

Chlorate, Chloride...should have written it down I suppose, not that I wanted to give anyone a heart attack.

"Wouldn't they have found that at a post-mortem?"

"Probably, I don't know and I didn't care. As it turned out there wasn't one, someone having all the symptoms of a heart attack in front of a doctor who was apparently trying her best to save him wasn't considered suspicious enough to warrant a PM. Nobody noticed the needle mark, since I jabbed him with something else when I was pretending to help him."

"And now you're done?"

"Now I think I'm done in every sense. I've done what Quentin wanted, I don't think I have very long left. Would you like to see his book?"

I took it, needed as evidence. I didn't read it then, but I've read it plenty of times since. Poor little bastard. She gave me another little bottle of nicotine that she'd never got round to using, and I kept that safe too.

"So what happens now, Inspector? Handcuffs and the Black Maria I assume?"

"I'll need to talk to Superintendent Watkins, get the warrant and I assume he'll want to send some of his officers to make the arrest. I'll be back tomorrow, don't leave town."

"Thank you, Inspector, I won't be going anywhere."

I never did talk to Watkins, and I never did go back

there. I read in that week's *Barry And District* that Doctor Sheila Grace Cooper had been found dead in suspicious circumstances at her home. Police had ruled out foul play and were not looking for anyone else in connection with her death, which is what they generally said when they thought someone had topped themselves.

Jane told me it was an injection of morphine, but that the cancer would probably have seen her off in a month or two. I might have guessed from how bright her eyes were, I've discovered since that it's often a bad sign. I'll let you decide whether I told Jane why I'd asked.

Quentin's book is in the envelope with this tape as you've no doubt discovered. You'll be the first ones to read it in nearly forty years. Make what use of it you like, must have taken the poor sod ages to write it all in that exercise book. Just imagine what his mother felt, reading it all those years later and thinking how she'd failed him. No excuse for murder of course, or for my not arresting her, though she wouldn't have lived to stand trial. You'll probably want to know why I didn't arrest her there and then…but I'm not around to ask, am I?

So, a case that started with a suicide is going to end with one. I'm done with it all. Jane's gone and I'm slowly going so I'll be hastening the process along a little. The doctor said Jane died of a heart attack, but they might find out the truth before too long. I couldn't bear to see her like that, and it was quick. That little bottle is still potent after all those years. I'm hoping it'll be quick for me too.

So, it's goodbye from a sad old fool whose time is done and who the world passed by long ago. When I take the stuff, I'm going to close my eyes and see two young people on Porthcawl beach, a fine upstanding figure of a man, and a beautiful dark-haired Welsh girl in her bikini, running back from the sea together.

Not a care in the world.

All the best, young man.

Other books by Andrew Peters

The Blues Detective
A Case For The Blues Detective
A Shot For The Blues Detective

The Barry Island Murders
Joe Soap

Solos
Monophonic

Check my Amazon Page for more, including short stories.

Thank you

Printed in Great Britain
by Amazon

26333702R00106